Hartmut

PLAN B

COLD WAR ADVENTURES OF A WEST GERMAN SOLDIER

Dedication

I dedicate this book to my deceased comrades and all those who gave their lives during the Cold War to protect the Federal Republic of Germany and its citizens. Their sacrifices and dedication shall never be forgotten!

Hartmut Schober

Foreword

My name is Hartmut Schober. I was a soldier at a time when a wall divided the German capital, and the so-called Iron Curtain divided Europe into two blocs, facing each other, lurking and bristling with weapons. As a German Bundeswehr soldier, I experienced the end of this historic era called the Cold War which, to the good fortune of all of us, dissolved peacefully instead of leading to an armed conflict. One such conflict would have undoubtedly turned the whole of Europe – and Germany in particular – into a field of rubble.

I am delighted that I have been given the opportunity to tell my story – with the kind support of Tom Zola. He helped me with my literary debut. We are both united in the desire to make military service understandable to those who have not served. We want to show what it is like and what it was like. The Bundeswehr can always count on public interest when the media trumpets the next scandal. Still, the ordinary soldier's everyday life, the usual insanity of the German soldiers' daily business, is beyond general recognition. I was a conscript and am still active as a reservist today. Unfortunately, a career as a "lifer" was denied to me, as you will read later on. Thus, I cannot provide you with live combat stories, neither in Afghanistan, nor in Kosovo, nor with the Navy. But what I can do is give the reader insights into the Cold War's final phase and what it was like to be in military service during this time. Even though the following story may cause some readers to doubt some incidents' authenticity, I can assure you that all of them occurred just that way. From today's point of view, the training practices described may seem inappropriate, at times even cruel. Still, during those days, they were part of the everyday life of the troops. After all, we "fought" the Cold War. The threat from the East was real and omnipresent, and it affected the West German soldiers' attitude and behavior at that time. Even though politicians nowadays like to claim otherwise, in my humble opinion, we soldiers of the German Armed Forces saw ourselves standing in the tradition of the Wehrmacht in terms of enthusiasm, honor, comradeship, and fighting spirit; and we were consistently and constantly confronted with the gigantic armies of the Warsaw Pact. George Washington is credited with saying: "To be prepared for war is one of the most effective means of preserving peace."

A motto I can relate to and appreciate.

Of course, not all soldiers had the same experiences back then, at the end of the '80s. Still, I think that many of my contemporaries will see themselves in my story. Readers from future generations may disbelieve and frown at the German soldiers' hard life at that time, just as those older than me may smile and shake their heads about my kid-glove military training in contrast to their own in the '70s, 60's or earlier. I guess this is just the way things go.

The Bundeswehr, in any case, was and is a universe of its own, and my story shows only one of many facets. Out of conviction, I can say that I enjoyed being a soldier, even though I was very, very close to despair more than once.

The speech of my first *Spiess* on my very first day of military service always comes to my mind: "Men, the next few weeks won't be easy! But always remember, tough times go by, tough guys don't. Any gardener can confirm: Only the hard come into the garden!" ... which is just a silly German adage saying you have to be tough to get somewhere. Many may dismiss that as a hollow, stupid saying, but somehow it helped.

In my narrative, I exclude lengthy descriptions of drill command training and other things known to anyone who has completed military service or served or is serving as a temporary or professional soldier to avoid boring anyone. I'll confine myself to the highlights. This can cause a distorted picture of military training in uninformed readers, which I will not leave unmentioned. I intend to share my experiences with others so that they may realize, too, that reality can surpass fantasy when it comes to the unbelievable. However, I have changed personal names and some names of places.

Finally, a word to those who recognize themselves in my text: "Sorry, *Kameraden*, but the stories are too good not to be told!"

Plan B – this is my story.

One final note: Please check the glossary for more information whenever you stumble across a term or reference that you do not understand.

Prologue

There are moments in life when I wonder how I arrived at this particular point of my existence. Sitting under a table in a pub of a suburb of Cologne and clinging to one of the table legs, that time had come again. I could feel my three comrades at my back, each hugging one of the table legs. When splinters flew around my ears from a wooden chair that had hit our table by happenstance, a thought came to me that I'd rather be somewhere else now.

How the hell did I get in here in the first place?

In my mind's eye, the eventful past months came to life ...

An Unexpected Encounter

It all started with my mustering.

Who am I?

My name is Hartmut Schober. I was born in 1971 in Ludwigsburg and, at the time, I was a journeyman in electrical installation. Shortly before my journeyman's examination, I received the invitation for mustering. At the end of the '80s, the Cold War had long since passed its climax, and Bonn was the capital of the Federal Republic of Germany (you may know it as West Germany). On television, *Miami Vice*, *Magnum*, and the famous German *Commissioner Schimanski* courted the audience's favor. We still paid with the Deutsche Mark and the radio played pop music by very young artists like Madonna and Kim Wilde. Germany was divided in two and, unfortunately, I belonged to a year-group of low birthrates.

So, nobody gets away with anything!

There was still general conscription in 1971; the fatherland had to be defended against the Warsaw Pact's wild hordes. Refusing was not an option for me anyway because my family had made their men available for military service since the Romans had tried to gain a foothold in Germania. My ancestors had served mainly in the Uhlans and the Jägers, typical units for the old garrison town of Ludwigsburg. Furthermore, we have musketeers, grenadiers, mountain rangers, paratroopers, and an air force sergeant in the family, so we are pretty versatile on this point.

We even exported a few family members overseas, just in time to start quarreling in the bloody American Civil War.

The American branch of my people remained committed to the family tradition. So, we also provided soldiers for military action in Korea and Vietnam. And we are still doing so in the current conflicts.

One of my US relatives served in the air cavalry and was involved in this new service branch's first combat mission during the Vietnam War. This mission took place in the Ia Drang Valley. Some readers may be familiar with it from the feature film *We Were Soldiers* starring Mel Gibson. You can find the name of my relative who died there in the credits of the movie and the Vietnam Veterans Memorial.

In any case, I felt a particular obligation to make my contribution to the family tradition. Suppose I had dared to refuse joining the military. In that case, I could have started to look for a new clan, that much was clear – nobody had told me that openly, but it was virtually an unwritten law. Not that I was going to refuse ... I was raised pretty conservatively after all.

Early on, I had been allowed to listen to my grandfathers' and great uncles' war stories and had thus learned of the fate of the fallen and missing family members. And my father and my uncles contributed wild stories from their time in the *Bund*. As a child, I also enjoyed war toys and toy weapons, not only during carnival time! Yes, that's how it was back then; almost all the boys played with plastic tanks and fake weapons – except, of course, for those who attended Waldorf Education schools and danced their names there. As a rule, they were only allowed to deal with wooden toys without any reference to violence.

On the other hand, I was practically born into the marksmen's club. I was already allowed to accompany other family members on hunting trips and to the shooting range during my youth. Uniforms and weapons were and are an integral part of my life.

The peace in Europe that has lasted since the end of World War II prevented more of our younger family members from doing military service – in addition to my father and me, there was the uncle mentioned above, who was an officer and a professional soldier, as well as a cousin who spent his *W15* time as a motorcycle messenger. Then some were (and still are) members of the German Military Reserve. All this taken together, it remains to be said that my path to Bundeswehr was practically predetermined.

But back to my mustering-in.

On that day, I was punctual, as I always am, arriving at the local draft office, which at that time was in an old barracks building with an impressive warrior relief above the entrance, in front of it waving the flag of our Federal Republic of Germany on a long mast. I remember as if it had been yesterday. The picture of the black-red-gold cloth in front of the simple, functional building is still very much alive in my mind. My young self was impressed ... and intimidated. What else could I do but enter?

By the way, does anyone wonder why German is such a weird language? The German word for local draft office is *Kreiswehrersatzamt*. Try saying that out loud.

Anyway, I registered with the porter, who forwarded me to the check-in desk, where a clipboard was given to me. I entered my personal data on it, and I was also asked to specify any assignment requests. I only expressed one heartfelt wish in this field: to be close to home.

Others dreamed of becoming pilots, UDT divers, submariners, or paratroopers. The Bundeswehr could immediately make me happy if they didn't send me too far away from Ludwigsburg. If it were granted, my wish would inevitably lead to the infantry – or the tank troops – but I was probably too big for the old tin cans. At least that's what I heard.

The clipboard questionnaire also asked me the following question: "Do you want to refuse military service?" This inquiry drove me mad, so I wrote: "I am an alternative civilian service refusenik!"

*

After everyone in my muster call, all ten of us, had shown up, we were called one at a time to an official in an adjacent office. He went through the items on the questionnaire one by one with each of us. An evil premonition arose when my inquisitor frowned as he read my statements. He finally arrived at the question of refusing military service, visibly cut off reading any further, and pursed his lips.

"So," he went on without raising his voice. "So, you want to refuse military service?"

"No way," I replied indignantly. "I'm an alternative civilian service refusenik!"

He looked intently at the form in his hands, and I could literally see the gears rattling in his agonized clerk's brain. I had trouble suppressing my laughter. The above dialogue repeated twice before the guy apologized and left his office – almost hastily – to seek his superior's advice. Shortly afterward, I was allowed to get to know that superior myself; he stormed into the office and barked: "You look like one lovely joker! Clowns like you are particularly popular here!".

I shrugged my shoulders and looked at the two clerks with a trustworthy smile. Finally, I got my stamp on the form and was sent on for medical examination.

*

In the other wing of the building, it smelled pungently of disinfectant. The linoleum floor shone in the light of the fluorescent lamps. They instructed my comrades-to-be and me to take off our clothes and stow them in narrow metal lockers. Soon we found ourselves, bare except for our underwear, in the antechamber for the official medical examination. Over a loudspeaker, the medical personnel let us enter one after the other. I remember a handwritten note hanging at the door, urging me to accept the following examination, including the infamous palpating of the testicles, as a compelling necessity.

For this reason, please do not start a discussion about the meaningfulness of it. The end of the note expressed a hint that the said examination was no pleasure for the doctor either. We figured out what we were supposed to do, but we didn't talk to each other. The atmosphere around us was marked by a tension that had gripped us all. So, we remained silent, each keeping his thoughts to himself.

I was called, rose, and entered the exam room itself. Two ancient female doctors, close to apparent death, awaited me. The examination room exuded the charm of an old classroom and urgently needed renovation.

The examination progressed rapidly until finally that scanning of the testicles was imminent.

Just when I had my underpants hanging around my ankles – so I was completely exposed at the bottom – a civilian secretary entered, but without knocking first. To make things worse: I knew this young lady from my school days. I had been allowed to get to know her even better once ... very close, even! The doctor, holding my testicles in her hand, looked at my school friend in a piqued manner and noticed my involuntary body reaction to the unexpected encounter only at the last moment.

It was summer, my school friend wore a tight top and a short leather skirt, and as I said ... we knew each other in the Biblical sense.

Anyway, my school friend's expression slipped. The second doctor, the one brooding over my health record behind the desk, looked at the scene and burst into laughter. Their vulture-like cawing still echoes in my ears today.

Anyway, my friend simply dropped the file she was carrying, turned around on her heels, and disappeared from the treatment room. Good Heike still can't look at me at our regular class reunions without turning cherry red. We have never exchanged a single word about the incident.

Fill it to the Brim!

The examination ended with that unexpected encounter. I was passed on to the measurements office. A doctor's assistant was waiting for me, whom I towered over by two heads, with my 190 centimeters height (that's 6.2 inches).

She asked me to put myself under the body-height bar for sizing. The good lady tried, stretching and stretching, to reach the caliper gauge. Her efforts culminated in her climbing up on me, grabbing the slider, and pulling it down forcefully. She ended up crashing it onto my skull. I went groaning to my knees, and she went with me because she was still clinging to me. Closely entwined, we landed on the linoleum floor. Of course, another employee of the local draft office had to enter the room strictly at that moment!

I magically had all the bad luck that day.

"Am I interrupting?" the lady grinned and left the room laughing brightly.

At the second attempt, the small doctor's assistant climbed onto a chair, and lo and behold, the measurement went well. However, I wore a bump and headache from it as I left her office.

We continued with the urine test.

*

A middle-aged, resolute, even straightforwardly bossy female employee handed me a sample beaker with the words: "Fill it to the frigging brim!" A ghastly hiss sounded in every syllable. "There's no point in cheating! I can always see you through the mirror on the ceiling! So, don't even try!"

There were probably wise guys who tried to mix sugar cubes or vinegar in their urine to compromise the result and hopefully get a certificate of unfitness. With this one in your pocket, you could avoid military service and alternative civilian service.

To accuse us of trying to cheat was baseless on the face of it, but I found it outrageous, and so I decided to take the good lady at her word.

So, I filled the sample beaker up to the very rim!

The other poor guys saw this and, of course, did not want to stand back. In the end, ten brimful urine sample beakers were lined up on the tray, all of them nice and hand-hot. The beakers were really, really filled to their capacity; not a drop more would have fitted.

As we stood around the waiting room in front of the mustering commission's offices, ready for the following item on the agenda, we heard loud nagging and ranting from the direction of the urine-sampling room. It had to be impossible to move our samples without making a mess. The poor woman was informing the entire building wing of this.

An elderly gentleman in a white coat then waltzed into the waiting room, looked at us squeaking in hilarity, and asked us to refrain from any further jokes. Turns out he was the attending in charge.

We were finally called one by one to the mustering commission's room, a truly intimidating encounter!

I found myself in a large chamber; the combined scent of cleaning agents on the cold linoleum floor, aftershave, and mustiness rose to assault my nose. The commission members were enthroned on a raised dais behind white cafeteria tables, the metal frames of which were coated with greyish powder, and all of them looked down on me with great solemnity. Our Federal Republic's flag, black-red-gold bars with the national eagle superimposed, was stretched over the wall behind them.

I felt like a midget at that moment.

The chairman asked for my personal details before announcing the verdict, which was more than clear: Fit for duty! A date for an ability test to follow!

My Fate Called for Jäger Troop

The ability test took place a short time later in Stuttgart, more precisely in the local draft office on the Pragsattel. The Prag is a ridge north of the Stuttgart city center between Killesberg Park and Rosenstein Park. The district bordering the North Station and the Prag Cemetery in the west bears the name Auf der Prag and belongs to the district of Northern Stuttgart. As I learned years later, the entire Pragsattel is honeycombed with bunkers. One very deep bunker is located exactly under the local draft office. The communication center of the then Stuttgart-based high command of Military District V was located in that bunker. I found this odd since I'd driven across the Prag countless times without ever suspecting what might be hidden beneath the earth.

There is another, more famous, high-rise bunker in Stuttgart. I am talking about the so-called *Bosch Tower*. It was built in the Second World War. The sizeable German engineering and electronics company Bosch had displayed its advertisement on its walls until 2013. It is still called *Bosch Tower* by the people of Stuttgart.

The ability test, divided into different tasks, did not present me with any particular challenges but came up with some surprises. It said that I am very talented in aircraft recognition and that I am also good at technical matters and teamwork.

After the test, I chose from a wide range of positions within the different military branches. But I remained true to my wish. Now I waited impatiently for the call-up because I had a well-paid job at a well-known mechanical engineering company in prospect. As I said, I had my journeyman's certificate in my pocket, as well as my driver's license. Now all that was missing was military service! It is worth noting that in my day, it was customary for male applicants to be asked first and foremost about their military service in job interviews. If the service record was still missing, we were immediately told: "Thank you for your interest, please get back to me after your time in the Bundeswehr." The firms feared that, otherwise, the armed forces would oblige employees to quit once they were drafted.

Fortunately, I had been able to negotiate a deal with the engineering company's HR manager in question. He would save me a position for the time of my military service if I promised to do it as quickly as possible.

Consequently, I had to scribble on a lot of paper and make the telephone lines glow until I finally hassled the people to call me in promptly. The low birth rate of my year and the resulting shortage of personnel probably helped me with my project. There were more quitters and refuseniks than usual in my time. The military service was therefore increased to 18 months, just in time for my year!

When the conscription notification finally reached me, I read it with a great deal of excitement. It started ... I was destined for the Jäger troop.

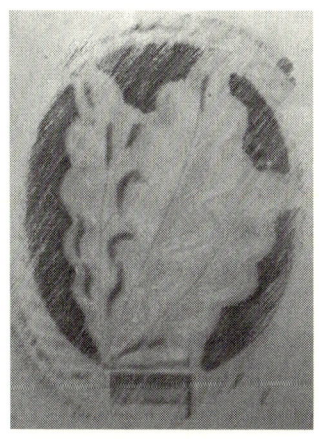

Day 1

My father dropped me off at the barracks gate on the first day of my military career. There I was, armed with a sports bag, my papers, and a queasy feeling in my stomach. A tall guy, slender, a bit lanky, with water-blue eyes and a short, red-blond head of hair, joined me. He was about my age and would soon become a good friend. We greeted each other somewhat reservedly and introduced ourselves.

I learned that he came from near Ludwigsburg, from a small town in the same county.

His name was Frank Bässler.

More conscripts, primarily young and still wet behind the ears – a description that naturally also applied to me at that time – joined us. Soon there were so many that we formed a big cluster of men. The soldier standing next to the barrier guarding the gate seemed increasingly nervous because of the large crowd in front of the barracks. Some time passed by before we, as a group, summoned up our courage and strode toward him.

What followed was the usual procedure: the greeting, the first meal in the mess hall, still in civilian clothes and disparagingly regarded by all the men in uniform. Afterward, we went to be issued uniforms. Following the herd and driven by grim *Unteroffiziers* bellowing at the top of their lungs, we were measured and lavished with uniforms and material that we finally had to carry to the barracks. After arriving there, allocating us to barracks-rooms and beds was done by just-as-loud NCOs.

I was happy to discover that I shared a barracks-room with Frank. There we were, six in number, including Frank and me, who found ourselves in a tiny room, lined with wooden lockers and bunk beds, from whose thin tubular steel frames the paint flaked off. In the middle of the barracks-room stood a table and six chairs with worn seats. Under the window with single glazing, an ancient radiator rusted to itself. To describe the furnishings as "Spartan" would give it a recognition that it was not entitled to. Frank immediately made the observation that the furniture obviously dated from the Wehrmacht. To his luck, none of the instructors heard that! I remembered the old black-and-white pictures from my father's photo album that had been taken in his Bundeswehr barracks-room; these photos were 25 years old now. And they showed similar furniture that decorated my barracks-room – possibly even the very same.

The first thought that came to my mind: "Six strangers crammed into a tiny room. Can that work?"

Then a drill instructor kindly roared at me, instructing me to enter the names of us six in the occupancy list, which hung on a clipboard attached to the door. As I was told, I entered: Myself: Hartmut Schober, because it is rude to put yourself first. Then Frank Bässler. Next, Paul Kramer, a small German Russian with a black head of hair, had already done his military service in the Soviet Union with the Black Sea Fleet and then fled to the West. He did his Bundeswehr service with the honorable intention of serving his new homeland. He also hoped that compulsory military service would improve his knowledge of German.

Then we had Tasso Karasakis, a 20-year-old scalawag with a German mother and a Greek father. He had no desire for military service in the Greek armed forces and hoped to have a cushy slot at the *Bund*. Tasso was soon to receive the inglorious nickname "Cock Head," which was due to his already very pronounced bald head and a strange, elongated dent in the middle of the same. The bushy side hairs gave him an almost grotesque appearance. Of course, it would not remain so bushy for long. Tasso is remembered above all as someone who complained passionately about everything and everyone.

Bankwat Daechate, a wiry little Thai German, was the next one on the list. His German mother had put up a fuss when she had dropped him off in front of the barracks gate, which is why I had already noticed him there. She was a complete eco-dame in a hippie flower skirt, peasant blouse, and Jesus slippers. As if she was trying desperately to live up to every cliché, she drove a lemon-yellow Citroën 2CV. Unfortunately, her son didn't shine very brightly. On top of that, he was the worst slob I was ever allowed to experience. He had tried to refuse military service but had failed at the task – much to his mother's displeasure.

Finally, Peter Riesch from the nearby Black Forest; he was of a tranquil nature. He had hoped to be assigned to Calw as a paratrooper, which would have meant a shorter way home for him. Peter was attached to his animals and his parents' farm, especially the horses.

Well, there were six of us who were supposed to grow up into a sworn community: *barracks-room 02*. I still found the idea of sharing such a tiny room with these completely strange, shy-looking guys bizarre. I quickly got used to it. And as we soon realized, all six of us had dramatically underestimated what was ahead of us.

My family members always told me that the infantry was the "Queen of Battle," as we say in German. There even is a song of the same name.

Unfortunately, my dear family clan had concealed that this was probably meant ironically. Or I just hadn't noticed the irony. In any case, in my time, there was a general hierarchy in the Bundeswehr, starting with the military branches, and it worked something like this:

The nobles at sea, in the Navy,

the knights of the air, in the Air Force,

and the pesky bastards ... yes, they came to the army.

Now we were going to become Jägers, which by definition meant the light infantry.

The Jäger troop has a long tradition. Already by 1631, professional hunters and foresters had formed military units in the principality of Hesse-Kassel. Under King Frederick II of Prussia, also called Frederick the Great,

Jäger formations were established for the first time. His Prussian troops often got lost in their wars, so he hired the second- and third-born sons of hunters. (At that time, sons were still following their father's profession, but as a rule, only the first-born could take over his position, leaving the others empty-handed; this produced many young men with no future and no prospects.) So, *Old Fritz* killed several birds with one stone. The hunters' younger sons were allowed to engage themselves in his army and became highly motivated soldiers; they could shoot excellently and find their way even in rugged terrain. They were thus given professional prospects.

At Waterloo, Prussian Jägers played a decisive role in the victory over Napoleon. There is a famous story from the First World War of a French unit that mutinied when Württemberg Jägers moved into the trenches opposite them – the deadly precision with which the German Jäger corps used their rifles was notorious among the soldiers of the Entente and was often reflected in their loss figures. The French officers of that unit, in any case, had to have ten of their soldiers shot to restore order.

Throughout the centuries, German Jägers were regarded as well-trained soldiers who conspired to form an entity that functioned like clockwork. Even today, the Jägers are often counted among the elite of an army, and not without good reason.

As I said, the Jägers are infantrymen. And what is the infantry's preferred means of transport?

That's right.

The feet. This means marching, marching, and marching again, until blisters form upon blisters on their feet, which in turn form their *own* blisters. So, starting our basic training in a Jäger troop, we faced a physical challenge that should not be underestimated. I am not afraid to admit that the hard drills and field duties sometimes brought me to my very limits.

Going for a Ride with the CO

On the following day, my problems started. After a restless night in new surroundings, we had to line up in the early morning hours in uniform in front of the block. It was pitch dark, a fresh breeze blew the smell of mown grass around my nose, my eyes were still half-closed. One of the non-commissioned officers, a guy named Hungbauer who had the rank of sergeant, noticed that I was wearing civilian sneakers instead of boots, so he glanced at me angrily. I replied, somewhat intimidated by the still unfamiliar way of communicating, that I did not have any boots because my size (13) was not available. My answer satisfied him, and, for a few days, I wore sports shoes with the stone-grey-olive Bundeswehr uniform.

Three days later, I received my combat boots – and with them, the next problem. The quartermaster had only been able to find brown combat boots in my size. They came from an old stock of a type of boot that had been in use before. But at the end of the '80s, the Bundeswehr wore black at the base! So, I stood in a row with my *Kameraden*, who all had black boots on their feet. My brown kicks in the otherwise consistent formation attracted attention like an illuminated Christmas tree. They brought to the scene the same sergeant who had already glared at me because of the sneakers. He bestowed a dressing-down upon me, which meant nothing else than that he really gave me hell. Why had I come to destroy the beautiful image of his platoon with my brown boots, he demanded, spitting while shouting. I should have dyed my boots with black shoe polish, in his opinion! Who was I, this midget, waltzing around like that? He said he would squash me to fit in a hatbox without any problems. The fact that a sigh escaped me just seemed to spur him on even more. He roared and raved so that more saliva threads left his mouth and splashed around the area. I wished I was somewhere else, but I had to endure the tirades of the sergeant. When he had finally run out of steam, he asked me for an answer.

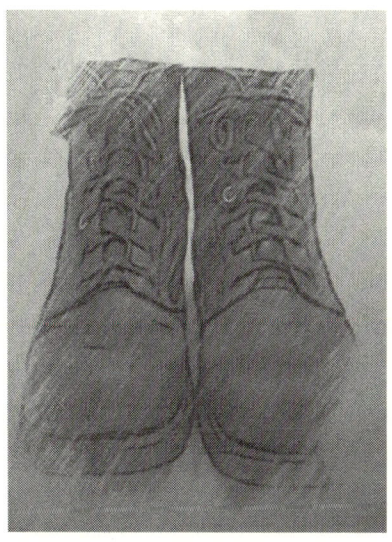

I objectively explained that dyeing the combat boots would permanently damage the leather and thus the boots. It was forbidden for me to damage the property of the Federal Republic of Germany. I knew that it had been quite usual in former Bundeswehr times to dye the boots, which had regularly led to a huge mess. I hoped the sergeant didn't know that. To my relief, he didn't. Somehow my explanations must have made sense to him. At least he calmed down. Then, he demanded I follow him to the *Spiess*, our senior NCO. I was allowed to explain the situation to him once more, whereupon he stood ponderously behind his desk and told us to follow him to the company commander. With this procession from office to the office, a more and more queasy feeling grew in me.

My fourth day with the military, and already I was on a ride to the CO… great!

The door to Major Steger's office was wide open. The *Spiess* knocked against the frame and saluted. It smelled of coffee and cake; the wall behind the desk was decorated with all kinds of framed course certificates and group photos. Out on the table to be admired were demilitarized cartridges of all calibers. Steger himself was always a calm, prudent, even friendly man with a massive mustache under his nose. His appearance inevitably made me think of the walrus Antje from NDR, the then-symbol of Northern German Broadcast. Steger also possessed the gift of putting people to sleep with his deep voice, which we recruits were able to experience, especially during his CO lessons. Again and again, some of us dozed off when Steger spoke and was then allowed to spend the rest of the lesson standing up. Despite everything, I never experienced a major screaming session – he even rebuked soldiers in a mannerly loudness. I remember him as a fair officer who always took time to listen to his subordinates.

Steger, in any case, rose, strolled around his desk, and greeted us all with a handshake – even me, the recruit, who in the eyes of many soldiers was not a full-fledged person.

Now I told the company commander the tired story of my brown boots. From the major's facial features, I could read that he was dismayed because time was stolen from him with such trifles. He looked at us, one after the other, and said in a neutral tone: "Gentlemen, I don't see any problem here. You simply stand in the back row with your brown combat boots when you line up, and nobody will notice. In the barracks-room, you can order brown shoe polish. You are very tall anyway and should be in the back." Then he turned to Sergeant Hungbauer and glared darkly at him. "Why did you put on such a circus for this, Herr Unteroffizier? I didn't expect such nonsense from you."

These last two sentences were sure to cause me some trouble ...

Hungbauer looked at me with hate and suppressed anger. It sent a shiver down my spine, but the CO and the *Spiess* were not interested in us anymore. Still, they were already chatting about the VfB Stuttgart game of the weekend.

When Hungbauer saluted again and stomped out of the office with me, it was clear that I had an arch-enemy from now on.

My Arch-Enemy

The hazing was not long in coming. Sergeant Hungbauer was known and feared as a bad grinder and manslayer. He always had to shellack us recruits. I still remember his most memorable lines:

"Leave the thinking to the horses; they have a bigger skull!"

"If I give you an order, I want you to do it at the double and yesterday!"

"When I order you to march in lockstep, move in complete sync with your comrades, you slanted thighs!"

"One can't even storm a pigsty with you wimps!"

"On weekends, you can lift heavy women, but here you can't even manage a few decent push-ups. With you lame heroes, there is nothing to write home about!"

"Why do you have to be able to disassemble your gun with a sack on your head and then reassemble it? Do you want to know? You're on the battlefield at night, and the Russians are waiting for you. Your weapon is malfunctioning! What are you going to do? Light a match or turn on your flashlight? Then you'll die of lead poisoning immediately, you empty bottle!"

"You want to be Jägers? You are only pitiful caricatures of soldiers. Old Fritz would roll over in his grave at the sight of you!"

Once a *laggard* asked how long we will continue to march. Hungbauer answered: "You will continue to march until I tell you that you no longer have to! If God had wanted you not to march, He would have given you wings, and you would be in the Air Force now!"

"Laggards" were recruits who had reported for duty sometime after us. That meant they were usually recruits who had not shown up for duty and had to be captured by the military police. The laggards, who were known to us as "quitters," were of course particularly popular with the instructors and were accordingly given the all-round carefree package: special services, particularly frequent checks of equipment, extra formal training and, at the slightest violation, reports and punitive duty of all kinds. Of course, such measures occasionally also affected the rest of us. Hungbauer was on me, which unfortunately meant that not only I, but the other recruits paid for as well. Fortunately, my fellow comrades didn't blame me; on the contrary Hungbauer managed to become the most hated NCO of our training company. He did not only harass our *Barracks-room 02*, but all recruits experienced his general hatred for human beings.

In the beginning, we tried to have a good relationship with him. Once, I offered him my canteen during a field exercise on a hot summer day. He nodded to me and took a strong sip but immediately spat everything out again and bawled at me: "Do you want to poison me? It tastes like rat piss!"

I had only filled my canteen with Posca, an old soldier's trick for quenching thirst. My grandfather taught me this. Posca is a mixture of two parts wine vinegar or apple vinegar and eight parts water. In the blazing heat of summer, there's nothing better!

At any rate, Hungbauer's conduct was grinding my gears. Yes, he was an NCO and I a recruit, but we were both humans at the end of the day, which he seemed to occasionally forget. Unfortunately, he never forgot which poor devil was responsible for him getting a going-over from the commanding officer ...

When the distribution of the weapons within our squad was up for discussion, he promptly assigned me to carry the MG, allegedly based on my height. Now I don't want to complain too much, but the MG3 gets really heavy if you have to carry it for umpteen kilometers. Little Paul Kramer was assigned to me like a pack mule (officially called 2nd gunner). I often had to take over the ammunition boxes myself in practice because Kramer couldn't cope with it. It wasn't him; he really did his best. Fortunately, our *Barracks-room 02* had already grown together into a sworn community, which is why we helped each other: We secretly emptied the ammunition boxes and packed the contents in each comrade's backpacks. So, Paul only had to carry the empty boxes and the spare barrel. I had enough to shoulder myself with my gun and all that other stuff. We got away with it for a while until Hungbauer got wind of it and started checking the ammunition boxes at every stop. But a solution was soon found for this as well. So, it always went back and forth. We became inventive in order to somehow worm our way out of the situation. The instructors, above all Sergeant Hungbauer, were on their guard to get to the bottom of our latest tricks.

I knew that the Wehrmacht had had practical carrying straps for the ammunition boxes from my grandfather's war stories. I'd never seen the same during my Bundeswehr time.

I spoke to our supply man in the armory about it one morning, but he showed little inclination to help out a recruit. He just shrugged his shoulders and said with a rich Lower Rhine patois: "Never heard of! We ain't have that. It's not on any of the lists either. And if it doesn't appear on my lists, there's no."

Alright, so that wasn't how to do it. One must know that the ammunition boxes of the MG3 of the Bundeswehr were almost identical to those of the Machine Gun 42 of the

Wehrmacht. Basically, they'd just been given a different coat of paint.

Then the International Arms and Collectors Trade Fair (ISA/IWB) immediately came to my mind. It took place annually at the Killesberg Exhibition Centre in nearby Stuttgart, including numerous military dealers from all over Europe. I knew from advertising posters hanging out in Ludwigsburg that this year's fair would open its doors next weekend. So, I arranged to meet Frank and Paul at Killesberg.

After the Winnenden school shooting in 2009, the fair was moved to Sinsheim, where it is still held annually today – unfortunately on a much smaller scale than back in the day. Stuttgart's city had imposed ever more significant hurdles on the organizers in the form of ludicrous officialism. Since then, dealers and hotels in Stuttgart have had to do without the excellent business of the ISA/IWB.

In fact, we found the carrying straps we were looking for on the display table of a Belgian dealer and could buy some well-preserved sets. We got the ticket and entrance fee back by selling some of the straps to our *Kameraden* of the other squads; in the end, there were even a few Deutsche Marks left for a case of beer.

In any case, the carrying straps proved to be very practical the following week. Suppose one linked the holders at the ends of a carrying strap through the upper carrying handles of two ammunition boxes. In that case, one could hang the belt around the neck, and the boxes hung, their weight evenly distributed, under the armpits. Alternatively, one strap per ammunition box could be used, hooked into the side handles. Then you just hung it over your shoulder like an ordinary bag. In any case, it was hands-free, and carrying was much more comfortable. Of course, Sergeant Hungbauer was unhappy that we were using privately procured equipment on duty. After all, we had equipped half the company with the straps. He barked at us terribly and wanted to forbid us to use them anymore. But we saw no point in leaving things in the locker that were available and made the soldier's life noticeably easier. Again, the dispute went up the chain, and again the sergeant got himself rebuked by the CO.

"You should encourage the ingenuity of the men instead of suppressing it," Steger said.

As expected, the following weeks were one long torment. Hungbauer projected his own misconduct onto us or did not understand what Steger was trying to tell him. In any case, the sergeant used the whole symphony of permitted punishments and some measures that were not permitted at that time to make life difficult for us. We recruits knew our rights only superficially. So, we ran lap after lap on the obstacle course, lifted weapons, equipment, and our tired bones over the climbing wall again and again until even the fittest among us lacked the strength to overcome the obstacles one more time. Hungbauer led us swaying pack of poor devils back to the barracks and had to loudly prod exhausted men entirely. Most of the time, we had to move in the "lowest way of walking," so we crawled through the training ground meadows and occasionally over the concrete parade ground until our elbows and knees bled. Hungbauer, of course, did not crawl along. He belonged to that breed of instructors who, although they talked big, never lifted a finger themselves. We were already speculating whether his backpack might only have been stuffed with a pillow while carrying 20 kilograms and more with us.

With Peter, the sergeant had also found a new victim, whom he increasingly attacked. Peter was possessed, as I said, of a very calm nature, virtually a textbook recruit. But he was nobody who could stand up to someone like *Unteroffizier* Hungbauer.

One morning Peter strolled with his hands in his pockets across the barrack yard towards the mess hall. Hungbauer saw this from his office, tore open the window, and yelled: "Are your socks slipping, or is your belt broken? Now get your hands out of your pockets, you rare stupid bird!".

On another occasion, Peter leaned with his back against the shooting range's sidewall while waiting for our turn. Behind us, the G3 combat rifles repeatedly fired, the noise dulled by our earplugs.

"Do you think the wall is dilapidated and must be supported? That's German workmanship; it doesn't need any help standing up, you giant horse," Hungbauer suddenly shouted. He had sneaked up on Peter like a tiger. To him, it was some sort of perverse delight to harass poor Peter.

Insults against subordinate soldiers were also not permitted; strictly speaking, Hungbauer even committed criminal offenses by insulting us, which did not stop him. But Peter was such a well-balanced person that he preferred to bear the felonies silently instead of facing the hassle an official complaint would cause.

Another time Hungbauer screamed at him: "Riesch! Are you a cruel man? Your magazines freeze to death!" The fastener of one of Peter's magazine pouches was open, but we were in midsummer.

And so it happened one after the other: "Have you shaved today, Riesch? You should get closer to the blade next time, you pig!"

"You've lost something, Riesch! And that's your speed! When I say now, I mean right now, you brain!"

"You're not in the German Federal Railroad sleeping car here, you windbag!"

"And when a thousand naked hookers dance around you, you stare clear straight ahead, you frog's eye."

"Yes, what? Chaplain or what? Yes, *Herr Unteroffizier*, that's what you are supposed to say, you punk!"

A dialogue between the two, at which I could hardly resist a laugh, similarly took place:

Hungbauer nagged: "Riesch?"

"Jo?"

"Joe is the name of a gay cowboy or a Texas bull, and I don't see horns on you, you mentally confused spatula!"

This saying was very popular with the instructors during my basic training. It was recited again and again in modified forms. It originated in the movie *Full Metal Jacket* by Stanley Kubrick, which was relatively new at that time and from which drill instructors have since copied their lines – which always seemed ridiculous to me. I already knew the flick's content from the previously published book The Short-Timers by Gustav Hasford. The film is based on it, but I like the book better than the celluloid version.

One day Hungbauer ordered us to dig foxholes. Of course, he used this opportunity for further harassment: "You always behave like wild boars, so be it! Get on the ground and dig in! And stay down! You can't perform a folk dance when under shelling, either! If you get up before I say it, I'll bawl you out!"

At that time, Hungbauer was promoted to *Stabsunteroffizier*, which only fired him up even more into harassing us. Under his direction, our field duty bivouacs were dominated by nightly alarm exercises and extra orientation marches, as well as sudden NBC exercises and the popular *fancy-dress ball*.

"Fancy-dress ball" was what we called a procedure in which we had to line up in all our different army uniforms in front of the barracks, over and over again. For example, we were first ordered to throw on our fatigue dresses. We then had only a few minutes to hurry to our lockers, put the fatigue dresses on, and hurry back to our starting position. Hungbauer meticulously checked everything for fit and order according to the dress regulations. Then he ordered us to put on another uniform, and the thing started all over again. It could take a while until we had gone through all our outfits in this way: combat uniform with and without NBC protective gear, dress uniform, full dress uniform, PT outfit, swimming trunks, et cetera. One could imagine what the barracks-room looked like after six men had torn their clothes out of the lockers several times and in great haste and thrown everything back one over the other. So, the fancy-dress ball was obviously followed by a muster with locker inspection. Everything had to be clean and tidy according to the prescribed locker order.

The fancy-dress ball could be combined with other exercises at will, and Hungbauer did not lack imagination. I remember in the middle of the night, we wobbled back from a march, wet with sweat and exhausted, where a grinning Sergeant Hungbauer took over from the other drill instructors and immediately specified the first uniform he wanted to see. That was a good grind.

Hungbauer's specialty was to check everything for cleanliness by using his white cotton gloves. Wearing them, he inspected the neck of our water bottles from the inside as well as the outside; he checked on and behind lockers, on top of the door leaves and door frames, and along with the window frames. If he found dirt – even just a grain of dust – disciplinary measures hailed down on us poor recruits. As a consequence, the following weekend was done for – which unfortunately happened quite often. We called the additional services on Saturdays and Sundays *fire watch*, where, apart from occasional walks across the compound, we squatted in our barracks-room while always having our *sniffing bags* (our nickname for our gas masks) and *steel hats* (our nickname for our combat helmets) ready to hand in case the alarm went off – no matter if it would be only a drill or a real alarm. Listening to the radio was forbidden during such duties. Watching television was also forbidden. So, I always had something to read with me because that was allowed. During that time, I developed a predilection for science fiction literature, which was then available in quantity in cheap paperbacks. I left a not inconsiderable part of my pay at the train station's bookstore. During my basic training, I devoured works by greats such as Asimov, Heinlein, and

K.H. Scheer and old classics, for example, by Jules Verne. I also consumed pulp magazines, which were called *penny books* in the '80s. I preferred western novellas like *Captain Concho* or *Fort Aldamo*, but I also liked the good old *Landser* stories. In my despair, at some point, I read everything I could get my hands on. It was amazing how much you can read away when you have endless time I had during my weekend duties.

It should also be mentioned that Sergeant Hungbauer was an army-head through and through, who did not even know how to write "private life." He spent the weekends in the barracks, supervising and pestering the recruits on duty. So, he also scared our *Barracks-room 02* up every now and then during our fire watches and tortured us with senseless tasks like cleaning long-ago shining bright corridors and bathroom units, as if he believed that otherwise, we were likely to die of boredom.

What are you gonna do? It'll all pass, including basic training.

Our platoon leader had never slowed Hungbauer down; on the contrary, he seemed happy to have such a capable man under him, who let off steam on the recruits all day long. The other squad leaders and instructors also appreciated the omnipresence of Hungbauer and liked to make themselves scarce. So, they could do what Tasso had had in mind for himself: take it easy. Our Cock Head, on the other hand, had long understood that the life of a Jäger was not a quiet one.

The Nuclear New Year's Eve Firecracker

Despite all the exertions, I also connect a series of beautiful memories with my basic training in the Bundeswehr. For example, our day trip to the *Scientific Collection of Defence Engineering Specimens* in Koblenz was a memorable event. One can marvel at a vast collection of handguns, military vehicles, and tanks there. One day is basically much too short to admire all the collection exhibits, but our day trip was impressive nevertheless. The exhibition documents the development of weapons and other military technology, and I heartily recommend a visit. The *Scientific Collection of Defence Engineering Specimens* in Koblenz is more than just a museum; it is the German armed forces' long-term memory.

Moreover, a surprisingly scheduled NBC exercise during one of our field duties became a lovely memory to me. We were given the scenario by one of the instructors: that a nuclear bomb was about to be dropped. We went into position and waited for a Tornado combat aircraft to fly over our military training area and drop a practice bomb.

We waited and waited, but nothing happened.

Three hours deployed in the countryside, some of us had nodded off in our foxholes in the meantime, which – thank God – none of the squad leaders noticed. We suddenly heard a soft humming in the distance, which became louder by the second. A MAN 630, an old truck with a long snout, came up and stopped 50 meters away from our trench. I already knew that MAN truck type, called *Emma*, from photos taken during my father's military service. In any case, two figures got out, dropped the tailgate, and rolled down an orange barrel. They removed the lid, threw something into it, got back into their truck very quickly, and left. We stretched out of our respective holes in our trench and tried to catch a glimpse of the barrel standing in the fern. Soon orange smoke rose from it. That was supposed to simulate a mushroom cloud. Fascinated, we stared at the smokescreen that spread across the clearing when the lieutenant of the NBC troop who was responsible for the exercise came running up energetically and repeatedly yelled, "NBC alert!"

"Put on masks and protective gear, then pick up your weapons," the squad leaders ordered loudly. "Immediately after a nuclear attack, we have to expect an enemy attack!"

Now a hectic bustle broke out among us recruits. We ran around like chickens and squeezed into the sauna suits. The superiors were driving us on noisily. But you can't see much once you have the gas mask on your face. Because it was hot and humid on this summer day. The heat accumulated under the forest's leaves' roof; the masks' panes were also soon fogged. Therefore, collecting our weapons turned into a slapstick interlude. Several G3 rifles fell to the ground, clattering. While some of us were still getting ourselves into the protective gear, others ran into each other blindly. Frank stumbled across a branch and disappeared into a sea of stinging nettles. After five minutes, we were everything but combat-ready. The instructors tried to keep their facial expressions calm. The lieutenant ended the exercise annoyed and called his superior via radio, a first lieutenant who immediately came up in his *Volkswagen Iltis*. He assembled us and used his car as a stage to talk to us. That's how he announced the radiation death of the entire company. Never before had he experienced such a mess, he told us, which above all made rage veins stand up on the foreheads of our instructors, as our poor level of training ultimately fell back on them.

In fact, I think that the squad leaders had hardly or not at all prepared us for this NBC exercise. Hungbauer and others were far too busy torturing us to have found the time to teach us something valuable. Furthermore, I still wonder today what this New Year's Eve firecracker, just 50 meters away from us, should be at all. If it had been an actual nuclear explosion, one wouldn't even have found enough of us to bury in a matchbox. However, for a simulation, the alert could have been triggered instead of letting us wait until the NBC dudes finally came around to ignite their ridiculous banger. But what did Sergeant Hungbauer use to say?

"Leave the thinking to the horses; they have a bigger skull!"

In general, the NBC training was still pervasive in my time; one should not forget that a Russian nuclear first strike was treated as a possible option in the case of war. So, we practiced coping with the bulky protective gear and masks in all situations. This included an exercise simulating the replacement of a used filter. For this purpose, an instructor led us to a gas chamber, which was nothing more than a prefabricated garage with a metal door. Each squad had to line up inside in a circle with masks on. The instructor closed the door and introduced tear gas into the chamber. The gas filled the chamber within seconds, after which the instructor commanded us to exchange filters, meaning: hold your breath, unscrew your mask filter, and hand it clockwise to the next man.

Simultaneously, one had to hope that the comrade to the right did not take too long to remove his filter and pass it on. By the way, it was pitch dark in the small chamber, which didn't make the whole thing any easier. I was already turning blue in the face, a stinging emptiness convulsing my lungs when I finally received my neighbor's filter and screwed it on in a hurry. That really was high time! Because of the darkness, some people missed the filter they were handed. It fell to the ground, and while desperately scanning the floor, they ran out of air in their lungs. In this case, the affected soldier had to knock on the metal door and was let out. He spent the next few hours struggling with the aftereffects of the tear gas. Regularly after the exercise, the whole squad lay on the floor, choking and gasping. At least for our instructors, it was a lot of fun.

Battle in the Forest Corridor

In my day, the Bundeswehr, together with its allies, held regular large-scale exercises to deter the Warsaw Pact. Our training company also took part in such a maneuver, and another fiasco was to take place. Actually, it was not intended to use us recruits on such exercises at all. Still, some office-sitter from headquarters was enlightened with a glorious idea. So, we performed backup tasks on the sidelines of events. For this purpose, we went into position at a forest edge, which we had to secure against enemy forces. They were supposed to lay opposite us in just another piece of forest, about 200 to 250 meters away from us. A corridor littered with groups of bushes separated us from the "enemy."

During the exercise, our platoon leader was blessed with the magnificent idea not just to passively wait in position, as he was ordered, but to actively engage in reconnaissance in the forest in front of us. Thus, he directed me to command our reconnaissance party while it was making its way through the corridor. As a reminder: I was the machine gunner. Paul and I had dug ourselves in on the right flank of our area of responsibility, from where we had a good view over the whole site. We made our shooting iron, affectionately called *Susie*, combat-ready. On the left flank of our platoon, another machine gun was in position, which enabled us to take under crossfire any hostiles who showed up in the corridor. Our foxhole was filled with blank ammo almost to the upper edge, so we were prepared for all eventualities.

The platoon leader himself took command of the reconnaissance party. He ordered to consist of considerably more soldiers than were usually deployed on such a patrol. I suppose he wanted to prove his field commander qualities. Our comrades advanced across the corridor in squad formation. They labored their way through the rows of bushes while looking out for enemies. So far, the thing seemed to go by the book when suddenly two Alpha Jets flew over our area of responsibility. Their engines caused a terrible roar. Somewhere in the opposite woods, but far outside our vision, rapid-fire weapons opened up. Our *Kameraden* in the reconnaissance party on the corridor took full cover in the bushes. The racket kept on booming and rapidly increasing in intensity.

Then five anti-tank helicopters type BO-105 appeared above the treetops and swept over our heads, flying nap of the earth and directly along the forest corridor.

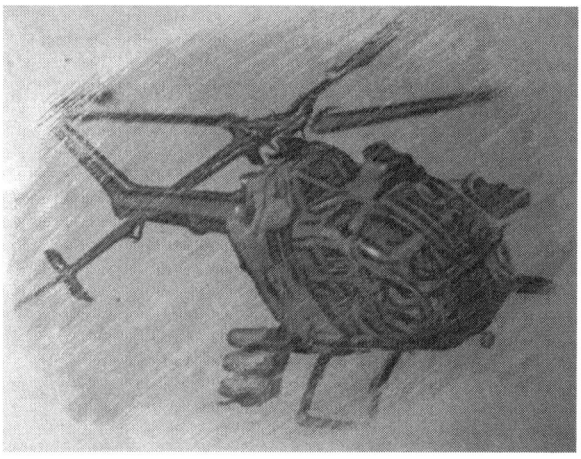

Just at this moment, two perfectly camouflaged Flakpanzer Gepard 1A2, German anti-aircraft tanks, which we had overlooked entirely until then and whose crews must have wriggled with joy when witnessing our reconnaissance party blundering naively across the forest aisle, broke out of their positions in the forest opposite us.

The Gepards' 35-millimeter Oerlikon-KDA L/90 twin machine guns immediately started to fire, causing a hell of a noise that even made my ears ring. However, I was 250 meters away from the magic! My comrades out there in the forest corridor lay convulsed on the ground and, screaming and whimpering in desperation, pressed their hands against their ears with all their might. And the whole thing was far from over. We had unexpectedly got into the center of a battle. Our side had reconnoitered the hostile anti-aircraft gun tanks with the Alpha jets and immediately took countermeasures. The helicopters turned around to initiate the hunt for the enemy Gepards. At the same time, a mixed battle formation consisting of Leopard 1A5 battle tanks and mechanized infantry mounted on Marder 1A2 fighting vehicles stormed the corridor. They rolled over the battlefield on rattling tracks that cracked the undergrowth and mowed it down. And suddenly, they opened fire, too. One of the Gepards lowered its pair of barrels, swung the turret, and commenced ground target bombardment, taking under fire the Leopard tanks which had arrived so abruptly. And my comrades were in the middle of this infernal spectacle!

Even if it was only blank practice ammunition, the shelling caused a terrible noise, and the air pressure beat against those poor bastards from the reconnaissance party. They could do nothing but press their bodies against the ground, feeling like cockroaches under the boot. Battle tanks, armored fighting vehicles, and anti-aircraft tanks leveled the underbrush on their advance. On the faces of my comrades showed the abject fear of being overrun by that mighty machinery. The inexperienced civilian without any military knowledge has no idea what it's like when an armored tracked vehicle thunders past you. It's like encountering a rhino stampede. The earth trembles, and you feel the raw power emanating from those military behemoths. And high up, the helicopters hovered over the chaos, target-searching. The air was filled with gunsmoke, which also entered our forest and burned in my airways. It smelled like cordite, grease, and diesel. Paul and I looked at each other helplessly.

Finally, the exercise referees reacted and tried to stop the rolling attack. They waved their arms wildly, screaming their lungs out, shouting by megaphone and on all radio frequencies because my comrades in the corridor were in danger of their lives.

"Stop all actions! Stop all movements!"

Several red flares rose above the forest corridor – the arranged sign for ending the exercise. Gradually the parties involved understood what was on. Silence returned. Little by little, our recruits rose from their hiding places. They showed grey faces and appeared jittery and completely disturbed. Quite a few tank drivers were shocked at how close they had come with their heavy vehicles to those poor human beings. It was a miracle that there were no wounded – or even casualties!

For some of us, the whole exercise was finished – they had suffered tinnitus and were taken away for medical treatment. The referees and the instructors did not spare any criticism of our platoon leader, who had acted without orders. In actual war, nobody would have called off the attack; my comrades caught between tanks and helicopters would have been exposed to the danger of getting crushed by the tracked vehicles and the effects of live ammunition. On this day, we all became acutely aware of the risks of uncoordinated action and how quickly friendly fire can occur.

By the way, our platoon leader was transferred before we finished our basic training, to where I do not know. But it was probably not an advancement.

Leaving Training Company

The last days of basic training turned out to be a quiet time. The instructors gradually started to treat us as equal soldiers. After three hard months, we received our green aiguillette and were allowed to call ourselves full-fledged Jägers. And after Hungbauer's special treatment, nothing was going to throw us off track quickly. Our *Barracks-room 02* stayed together as a unit, which made us all very happy. We quickly settled into our new functions in the Jäger battalion in Ludwigsburg. The time of special training began to complete our set of abilities required of a Jäger. For me personally, a perfect and beautiful time began.

We received a wheat beer glass and a schnapps glass with our first name engraved for our new billet from our new company. We were pleased about this, as it finally showed us that we were no longer recruits but full-acknowledged soldiers. The glasses were deposited in the company's recreation room on a specially made wall shelf. After duty, the alcohol often flowed freely, which is probably not surprising. We were a bunch of young men locked up in the barracks and robbed of the possibility of coming out during the week or even hook up with the opposite sex. After some horrible alcohol excesses, which led to whole platoons being out of order because all their soldiers were completely incapacitated in their beds, the CO set the limit to one bottle of beer per man per day. Of course, we were only allowed to drink in our free time. The most imaginative minds among us grunts thought up tricks to circumvent the restrictions. A freshly transferred second lieutenant opened the broom closet and noticed a diesel canister – which, of course, had no business there. It was only when a fruity, pungent smell came to his nose that he realized that the canister was filled to the top with schnapps.

Our so-called "Pencil Warriors" devised the most ingenious tricks to be able to indulge in their excessive consumption of alcohol. Many of them were men who had been classified "low serviceable" like *T4* or *T5* but had nevertheless been drafted because of their age group low birth rate. They were assigned after basic training exclusively to light services such as orderly-room work ... and I tell you, some of them were odd characters! Some couldn't even walk straight ahead. But most of them could drink for four!

Some of our Pencil Warriors' offices were facing the outer street. Since the building was integrated into the barracks fence, all they had to do was open the window and put their hands through the bars, and they were in contact with the outside world. In this way, some of them got relatives or friends to supply them with all sorts of goods, which they then sold on to us – of course, at prices that ensured that none of the participants in this supply chain was left empty-handed.

Trade between soldiers is as old as the profession itself. Even the Roman legionaries did business with each other, as historians found out. Archaeologists examined the helmets of Roman soldiers, the inside of which was carved with their names and units. Based on this information, it can be documented that retirees resold their equipment to active soldiers. It is essential to know that the imperial Roman legionaries were the owners of their helmets, armor, and weapons. These did not belong to the state. When entering the legion, part of the pay was withheld until the value of the equipment received was settled. Many legionaries provided their equipment with ornaments, often made of gold or gemstones, some of them from war spoils. Helmets, swords and sword sheaths, daggers, dagger sheaths, shield bosses, and belts were extensively ornamented. Such decorated equipment functioned as a kind of pension insurance. Helmet finds, which at first were regarded as magnificent officer's helmets, turned out after extensive historical investigations to be the material pension funds of ordinary legionaries. At the end of their service, the Roman soldiers cashed in on their property by selling it to their fellow soldiers. The dark side of this system revealed itself on the battlefields, where legionaries plundered their own dead.

By now, the interested reader will have noticed that military history is of great fascination to me, which is why I am still interested in it today. Those who do not know history are doomed to repeat it – not a beautiful prospect when looking at the last centuries' history.

Trade among soldiers is a tradition, at any rate, and could not be stopped even by the Bundeswehr, even if the officers had tried to do so by strenuous enforcement of regulations.

The Suicidal Major

In my new company, I soon stood out as someone proficient with light weapons, which is why I quickly ascended to assistant trainer. My family has a long tradition as hunters and sport shooters, which brought me into contact with weapons of all kinds since my early youth. I learned to shoot from my grandfathers and uncles. My personal supreme commandment was to ensure safety at all times during shooting. This had become flesh and blood to me, or as one of my shooting teachers once put it: "You must always treat a weapon like a poisonous snake, even if it is not loaded. A moment of carelessness can mean death! Therefore, concentration must never decrease when handling weapons!"

I have always conducted shootings safe and sound by obeying this principle – and it was a perfect match for the Bundeswehr, which is also very committed to shooting safety. Every German soldier and former soldier knows the safety rituals that seem strange to outsiders, such as handing over counted ammunition cartridges and a predetermined wording for every action on the range.

Also, sport shooters and huntsmen obviously adhere to the crucial rules in handling weapons – the explanation for why, in Germany, almost no accidents occur with firearms. Crimes related to firearms are seldom carried out with legal and registered weapons. The problem is the illegal weapons, which nobody monitors. There are an estimated 20 million in the Federal Republic alone! It is; therefore, questionable what effect stricter arms laws could have on crime statistics. It is well known that criminals do not apply for a gun ownership card before robbing a petrol station or committing a murder.

My uncle, the professional soldier, had already given me access to reservist shooting before my time as a soldier. The same uncle cultivated friendly relations in Switzerland, where I was once allowed to take part in a combat shooting drill (prohibited outside the armed forces and police in Germany). All this had been before my basic training, which gave me an advantage over my comrades as far as the shooting was concerned, reflected in my scores on the shooting range. My superiors were also full of praise for my respectful handling of weapons of all sorts.

Unfortunately, Germany's strict laws and regulations mean that interested citizens and ambitious reservists cannot avoid a trip to Switzerland or the USA if they want to train in the combat-conditions use of their weapons outside military duty. Even shooting at human-like targets is prohibited for civilian shooters in Germany. Moreover, I am surprised at how little our state seems to trust its own citizens. Well-trained ex-soldiers who have handled automatic weapons and explosives in the Bundeswehr are no longer even considered able to handle a sporting pistol until tons of proofs have been produced, examinations and psychiatric tests carried out, a membership in an association proven, and a crazy paper war waged. Weapon owners have a tough life in Germany.

In any case, my previous knowledge ultimately earned me a position in the armory besides being an assistant trainer. I soon had to realize that you won't go places with our hackneyed rifles that had been polished a thousand times and whose barrels were beaten out. But no other weapons were assigned to us except for some brand-new ones in our inventory, but they were never allowed to be issued. We could have used them to earn the Golden Shooter's Cord, a special Bundeswehr award for outstanding marksmanship results. So we soldiers of the armory soon used a trick to be able to shoot with the new weapons: We used the rifle stock of an old weapon, and its identification number, with a new weapon mounted on it; and then after shooting restored everything to the way it had been. A pleasant side effect of this approach was that after returning from the shooting range, we were able to show clean weapons very quickly to our superiors. At the same time, we carried out the cleaning of the weapons actually used afterward in peace. If we had to deal with dirty rifles and we had superiors like "Hungbauer" breathing down our necks, a blitz cleaning could be done: In the armory, we had two aluminum transport boxes, one filled with cold cleaner, the other with gun grease. Dip the gun into the first box, move it back and forth a little, pull it out again and shake it, then let it dry, dip it into the second box, shake it and let it dry again with the barrel pointing downwards: Blitz cleaning done.

One advantage we enjoyed as armory personnel was the privilege of access to the firing range at any time to check the functioning of recently maintained guns. We used this for extensive shooting training. Fortunately, our direct superiors and the battalion's supply officers, who provided us with virtually unlimited quantities of ammunition, accommodated us unquestioningly. Of course, every single cartridge expended had to be recorded. That's how the Bundeswehr worked (and works). Who doesn't know the thousand-fold quote: "Handed over XY cartridges correctly," to which the counterpart immediately answers: "XY cartridges properly received." In the Bundeswehr, everything must be bureaucratically right.

I also remember that dealing with ammunition was a recurring source of strange incidents. Once a shooting supervisor reported a missing case – I would like to emphasize that I am talking about one case, or to be precise, one empty brass case of a cartridge and thus a completely harmless thing. Nevertheless, armed with rakes and crawling on all fours, we had to turn the whole shooting range inside out. After hours of unsuccessful searching, the commanding NCO came to the bright conclusion to count the cases again. It turned out that the supervisor had miscounted – a whole three times in a row. He was, by the way, our chaotic Bankwat, who did not like weapons or ammunition at all.

His very first live-fire exercise with the pistol P1, Bankwat got himself the so-called *P1 thumb*: If one holds the weapon too high, the sliding block tears the skin from the thumb of the shooter when it recoils after the discharge, which usually leaves a small scar or a permanently rough skin place. That exactly is *P1 thumb*.

Bankwat was always a danger to himself and his comrades when dealing with weapons. He once forgot the protective gloves during a machine gun exercise when he had to change the red-hot barrel. He burned his paws terribly. While throwing practice hand grenades, he threw the first pineapple much too short. The trainer demanded that he put more strength into the next toss. But the failure had made Bankwat nervous. He pulled the second grenade out of his pocket, became more and more agitated, and finally did not throw it straight ahead towards his cardboard characters on the range but diagonally to it. The grenade hit spruce so far off the range-lane that it bounced back and landed immediately in front of the hip-high concrete cover for the thrower. Bankwat and the instructor made a heroic high jump into the protection of the cover, but the grenade didn't pop. In the excitement, Bankwat had utterly forgotten to pull the safety pin. Needless to say, he never got his hands on a live hand grenade.

In another exercise with the MG, a fox appeared on the shooting range.

"No one shoots at the poor animal!" roared the commanding NCO, but Bankwat pulled the trigger. As I said, he wasn't necessarily a luminary in the use of firearms. Probably the safest place was right in front of his gun when he was shooting. Earth fountains jumped up around the fox, but the animal remained unharmed. And the commanding NCO was on the verge of a meltdown.

At this time, one of my most bizarre experiences in the Bundeswehr took place: Some comrades and I were assigned to the shooting range again. This time, we waited in the trench in front of the targets for the commanding NCO's call to come out of cover and score the results. I was wholly absorbed in my thoughts, and through the hearing protection, I only perceived sounds in a muffled way. I was terrified when someone suddenly tapped me on the shoulder from behind. At my back was only the wall of the trench and then the shooting range above it. And there was still shooting going on! I whirled around and gazed in complete bewilderment into the face of a major who leaned down at me from the shooting range. He gestured for me to take off my hearing protection, which I did.

"Young man," he said with the serenity of a Tibetan monk. "Have you noticed? Hornets are all over this place!"

Speechless and with an open mouth, I stood there and was only able to shake my head.

The field telephone rang. The commanding NCO wanted to know what deranged idiot had climbed out of the trench in the middle of a shooting. I passed the handset of the phone on to the unknown major and said, "I think someone wants to talk to you."

"Major Lörcher on the phone," he reported. Listening to the commanding NCO for a moment, he then mumbled: "Ah, yeah, that's how it is. You can continue right away".

He gave me the handset back and left without a word.

We never found out what he was looking for at the shooting range target area.

Steel Wolf

It also happened when my comrades gave me my nickname, which is still attached to me today: *Steel Wolf* – *Stahlwolf* in German. Boredom can sometimes bear strange fruits, so in the countless hours of being on duty without any task, I embellished with some paint an MG3 case that had been tossed out as scrap. As the motif, I chose a predator mouth with fangs and eyes over it, like you'd see on airplanes. With fine brush strokes in red, white, and black, I painted it on the case. The shiny, heat-resistant varnish I used gave the object an almost martial appearance and reminded me of the muzzle of Disney's *Big Bad Wolf*.

We always had an MG3 with the bipod folded out on the steel cabinets behind the armory counter, which was never issued. To this weapon, I mounted the embellished case. Unfortunately, I neglected to photograph it and don't know what happened to the piece. In any event, the embellished case made my comrades associate me with a steel wolf. Et voila, my nickname, was born.

Pranks with Frank

Frank Bässler had developed into a reliable friend during the months of our service. Still, he was notorious for his fatal inclination to stupid jokes.

One of those jokes hit me on the day of our truck driving test. We still had one hour until the examiner's appointment, and I used the time to do my number 2 in peace. Frank knew very well that my morning sessions were sacred to me, and I preferred to have it quiet. I was just immersed in the sports section of the newspaper when I heard a rumble. Frank burst into the toilet anteroom and shouted at the top of his lungs: "Hartmut! Come quickly. The examiner is already here and raging because nobody is down at the vehicle!"

I dropped the newspaper in a panic and stormed, my trousers still at half-mast, out of the toilet stall ... and looked right into the faces of all my comrades loudly squeaking and beating their thighs with their fists. I would undoubtedly call Frank my best friend in the *Bund*, but I could have strangled him in such moments.

After we had accomplished getting our driver's licenses, we were often sent out to get supplies. One of these trips symbolizes the madness of procurement in the Bundeswehr, which is why I want to tell you about it: We reached the depot we were directed to and asked the way to the NCO in charge. In the hall, we met the man. And we couldn't believe our eyes. He lounged, his legs crossed on the tabletop of his desk, resting like a sheriff in the Wild West in his veranda chair. With a P1 pistol, he shot at spare glass chimneys of petrol lamps, neatly lined up on metal lockers opposite his desk. While he was reloading the pistol with plastic practice ammunition, a zealous private put new spare chimneys on the lockers. When the NCO – a sergeant – noticed us, he rose laboriously and approached us. We saluted him and handed him our shopping list. He told us that he needed some time to gather everything together; we should stretch our legs as long as possible. He then moved away. Meanwhile, I was so shocked by the scene that offered itself to me that I questioned the private about the "shooting exercises."

He grinned and replied: "Oh, it's the same every year. If anything is not consumed, the brass is gonna lower our funds next year. So, everything has to go, no matter how!" He laughed and added: "Yesterday we had a bonfire with three pallets of toilet paper."

Frank and I looked at each other in disbelief and could only shake our heads about such orgies of waste. The private, however, still seemed to be proud of it. At least his tone of voice sounded like he was.

Sometime later, by the way, that very sergeant gained sad fame because he taught a fresh second lieutenant, who was constantly tormenting and harassing him, a lesson with that very same plastic practice ammunition, but that is another story.

*

Occasionally Frank and I carried out transport missions for the local draft office by carrying files and the like. Frank had a crush on one of the nurses employed there. For this reason, we always contacted each other when such trips were on the agenda.

As I said, he had a penchant for joking at the expense of others, so he also made fun of the boys who had been mustered during our stays in the local draft office: Sometimes he would stand in uniform in the room of the nurse in question, looking into a file with a concerned expression on his face, and when such a poor bugger entered, he would casually give one of his sayings: "Well, here, we'll send him to the Navy! You like swimming, don't you?" Or also: "You go to the paratroopers. They have requested someone to test the parachutes. You got a good life insurance policy, don't you?" Also: "We'll turn you into a minesweeper. The pioneers have already announced their need again!" The classic was: "The German Air Force needs enthusiastic men to test the new ejection seats. Congratulations, you're in!"

Sometimes he just pointed to the vehicle we had come in, which was clearly visible outside the window, and told his victim that we were there to take him with us immediately. With his jokes, he chaffed a lot of recruits-to-be; some even came to tears. When I think of the faces of his victims, I still have to laugh.

Later Frank married the nurse and had two children with her.

*

During a supply trip that required us to pick up a load of live ammunition from a depot, Frank and I drove a 5-ton MAN truck. On the way back to Ludwigsburg, we passed by Frank's uncle in rural Schöckingen, respectively forced this "passing by" with a slight detour. We were early, and Frank had always raved about his aunt's cooking. Since we didn't feel like eating the usual chow hall food, we stopped at the next telephone booth and were invited for lunch. We parked the MAN behind the barn of Frank's uncle's farm.

After a decadent lunch and subsequently afternoon coffee, with which the aunt served delicious apple pie bonne femme, we started our way home, loaded with fresh farmer's bread, smoked meat, lard, and the remains of the cake. Unfortunately, after the afternoon coffee, Frank's uncle had uncorked the plum brandy, which we had all imbibed plenty of. To make it clear: We were pretty trashed.

Frank confused the forward gear with the reverse gear, which caused our ammo truck to land in the adjacent meadow. It immediately got stuck in the mud; we couldn't get out on our own. Calling the barracks and asking for help was not a good idea – we would have been treated with disciplinary measures, maybe even a stay in the arrest cells.

Anyway, swiftly, we were pretty clear-headed again! Frank asked his uncle for help. He was also very plowed and needed several attempts to make it onto his tractor at all. But with this, he was able to sort things out.

Now we had to hurry, it was getting dark already. Ludwigsburg was fortunately not far away. When we finally got back, the NCOs still gave us hell because the truck looked like shit.

*

Another time we had a flat tire with a Unimog truck. We were at the top of a steep road, which led down to a T-junction, where a telephone booth stood. I decided to call the barracks to announce our delay. So, I marched down the road while Frank and Bankwat started to change the tire. I went into the telephone booth, laboriously fiddled the coins into the slot, and called the barracks in Ludwigsburg. After I had put everything through and was about to hang up, I couldn't believe my eyes. A Unimog tire rolled past the phone booth at breakneck speed, burst through a small rustic fence, and crashed into the front window of a shop behind it.

I looked up the hill with my mouth open and saw my comrades grabbing their heads in horror. I ran to them, asked them what had happened. They told me: Frank had unmounted the flat tire by hand and called Bankwat, whom he had lost sight of so that he could then bring the spare tire over. Bankwat replied that he didn't know what Frank meant since he had put the tire right there behind him long ago. When Frank turned around, the tire was already on its way down. Bankwat had not put the tire "down" but placed it upright! The gradient of the road had contributed its part to the disaster.

The end of the song was that the cost of the shop window was deducted from our pay.

And shop windows are fucking expensive.

Those Happy Days

Our German-Greek comrade Tasso typically only got noticed for his complaints and moaning. Everyone had gotten used to it. There was little to nothing he couldn't fault.

As a rule, a courageous "shut the fuck up, Tasso!" or even a "sit, Tasso!" usually worked to silence him. But requests short of that, he always showed his appreciation with an arbitrary sequence of Greek curses.

But he had a tough time with our cookhouse hoss Max Huber with his nagging. Huber tolerated criticizing his food only to a minimal extent. The fact that he was a trained butcher and cook, and also had the dimensions of a Coca Cola machine, and was also a hobby boxer, as his broken and crooked nose testified, generally silenced any criticism of food in his presence. Now Huber was usually not present himself when the food was served. Our Tasso, therefore, believed himself to be in the safe zone when he began lamenting loudly at the food counter. He complained about the "gruesome pork fodder," called the lunch menu an "inedible stodge." "And in general, the portions are far too small! One cannot get enough of them!"

This last sentence was picked up by Huber, who had just entered the mess hall unscheduled. Slowly and like a nightmare personified, he approached our German Greek. It became quiet as a mouse in the whole mess hall; one could have heard a pinhead falling to the ground. At that point, it dawned on Cock Head that something was going awfully wrong. He was about to turn to Huber, but the cookhouse wallah put his arm around Tasso's neck and squeezed. Trapped in that death grip, Tasso was doomed to follow Huber to the food counter, where the cook reached into one of the warming containers, pulled out a handful of schnitzels, and put them into Tasso's mouth one by one. And you can say that they were pretty good schnitzels, nice and big, wide and tastily breaded. Tasso chewed hard so as not to choke.

But Huber raged: "You'll be full today! You'll be sated today, my friend!"

After introducing three or four schnitzels into Tasso, he reached for the ladle for the potato salad and began to feed him with it.

Tasso chewed like crazy for fear. When finally all he could do was choke, Huber finally let him go. Tasso went down on all fours and threw up. Huber was already there with a mop and bucket, of course. Cock Head was allowed to clean up the mess himself. Anyway, he never complained about the rations again. After this episode, he generally became a little more subdued and calmer.

*

In summary, I can say that this was my happiest time in the *Bund*.

I had good comrades, a task that occupied me, was stationed near home and had a good friend by my side. Soon, however, *Y-Tours* was going to take me somewhere else ...

Hit Between the Eyes

The end of my time with the Jäger troops came unexpectedly and suddenly during a two-week maneuver in which several NATO nations participated. The incidents there led to a caesura in my military service career.

The maneuver began unspectacularly.

We were declared the *Blue Force* and, as such, were to play the attackers. It was almost always like that. The attacker came from the west and wore blue armbands ... red armbands and coming from the east would have probably excited too many minds ... the referees wore, as always, white armbands.

We had been inserted into a small forest and were supposed to attack a neighboring grove at dawn, where an armored mortar unit of the US Army had dug itself in ... at least that was what the planners of the exercise had in mind. The choreography of those "battles" was always of prime importance to the brass. Basically, the winner was determined from the outset. Sharp tongues might call such exercises theater plays.

As far as the plan specified, the US Army troops had to repel our attack and throw us back, facilitated by the fact that they knew where we were and what we were up to. Besides, we (as the enemy in this case) were encouraged to play along with it.

So, we ground pounders set up our *dachshund garages*, as we called our Bundeswehr tents and our squad's bivouac places, and ate the rations from our EPA (one-man packs, which include food for one day). Since we were forbidden to make fire, we ate ravioli, chicken fricassee, noodles with chasseur, and so forth, cold. For protection, our platoon leader had a bunch of patrols march around in order to secure our area of responsibility.

Because the hardtacks from the EPA, which we called *armor plates*, caused me an upset stomach, I had to crawl out of my tent in the middle of the night. It could have been the tube cheese as well – disgusting stuff that is supposed to last for 100 years. Anyway, I grabbed my folding spade and a roll of toilet paper and set off, as quietly as possible, into the woods to look for a quiet place. I sneaked through the undergrowth; the view was sometimes more, sometimes less, due to the shining moon, which was intermittently covered by clouds. Tree trunks towered around me in the air like black columns. I could recognize at most the silhouettes of the branches. Since I didn't meet any of our patrols, I thought I was still inside our responsibility area. Then I suddenly heard muffled voices ahead but didn't understand a word.

That must be one of our patrols, I thought, and approached slowly. I didn't want to frighten my fellow soldiers and prepared to give the recognition password. Suddenly I came across a wall. Thoroughly irritated, I looked at the stone obstacle that ran through the forest and blocked my way. It wasn't very high; I stretched out a little and looked beyond it. It was only now that I realized that I had arrived at the enclosure of a farmstead, which was located north of our area of responsibility.

Boy, I got off track really good!

But I was even more surprised by the M106 mortar carrier, a box-shaped tracked vehicle that had been parked near the wall on the other side. I thought it was an M113 which is a very similar vehicle that the Bundeswehr possessed. Despite the semi-darkness, I could clearly see the barrel of the 120-millimeter mortar protruding from it. Also, the voices that I had heard before were coming from the interior of the vehicle. I understood now that they were talking in English. A cumulus cloud, which had pushed itself in front of the moon, at this moment moved further and let earth's satellite once again light up the site. In the moonlight, dozens of American soldiers became visible, lying in their sleeping bags, and dispersed over the whole farm property while they slept. Red armbands could be seen here and there. No tents, no guards around the camp; no one protected the "enemy's" position. My colleagues from overseas obviously slept like a log. The guys felt really safe here. At least our attack was planned for the following day and the Americans – or *Ami's*, as we Germans call them fondly – were not where they should have been.

But what should I do now?

Sneak back and risk getting caught by an American patrol after all? Well, that would undoubtedly have given people a good laugh!

German Jäger captured with a folding shovel and toilet paper!

It was a miracle of the first order that I had marched straight through the German and the American lines without falling into anyone's clutches. I'm sure it wouldn't work out again! On the other hand, I didn't have my rifle on me.

So again, what should I do now?

Then enlightenment came to me in the form of the idea of simply making use of my dear *Ami's*. They certainly had material with them that I could expropriate for a midnight requisition. Gently I laid down my spade and the toilet paper and climbed over the wall. Between this and the M106, I let myself down.

And bingo!

I found myself in front of stacked boxes filled with practice hand grenades. They were the same blue plastic pineapples with white powder fillings that we used. Quietly I fiddled around with the clasp of one box until it popped open. I took a whole load of grenades and put them in order on the loamy ground. Squatting, I grabbed the first one, pulled the safety pin, and threw it in a high arc to a point far away from the peacefully dreaming Americans – I wanted to scare them, not hurt them. I repeated the procedure and had distributed grenades all over the farm site before the first detonated within a few seconds. Unfortunately, it caused a slight accident. One pineapple collided with the antenna of the M106 and fell inside through an open hatch. An infernal bang followed. The mortar carrier's interior, which functioned like a resonance chamber, amplified the noise immeasurably so that it quickly drowned out the other explosions. One poor guy covered in white powder rose from the armored vehicle immediately afterward, whimpering in pain and covering his ears. According to the bar-shaped insignia, he was a lieutenant in the US Army. He looked like a doughnut glazed with frosting.

I quickly pulled myself up over the wall and let myself fall down again on the other side. In the twinkling of an eye, I jumped to my feet, grabbed my folding spade and the roll, and then I took to my heels. Hell-bent for leather, I rushed through the forest. Branches grazed me, wood and fir cones cracked under my boots. The darkness didn't stop me from doing a heck of a sprint. I ran, and I ran until one of our patrols stopped me with a peremptory challenge.

I gave the password right away and warned them to alarm the others immediately since the Americans were north of our own position and not far away, instead of being in the eastern forest area, as it was agreed upon. At first, the comrades stared at me in awe and then looked me over from top to bottom. Their gazes dubiously took in my appearance – the toilet paper roll shimmering in the moonlight and my folding spade. I think they thought I was out of my mind. Then, however, they remembered the noise that sounded through the forest from the north. The Americans – disoriented and startled – were utterly over the moon. That's how the patrol raised the alarm on the radio. As it quickly turned out, our entire company was already on its feet, because of course, everyone had heard the banging.

*

The following day, it came to light what had happened: The *Ami's* had simply made a mistake and had encamped in the wrong position. Anyway, reading a map didn't seem to be their strength. The responsible referee awarded me the destruction of the M106 as well as "killing" 15 Americans. The planned attack at dawn no longer took place, by the way. It wouldn't have made any sense!

But for me, the real trouble had just started. The American commander in charge wanted my head and demanded the most rigorous disciplinary measures. He actually wanted to see me in jail! The same applied to the planners of the maneuver, as I had destroyed their delicate battlefield choreography. The M106 was out of action for a long time because every slit was clogged with white powder. I very much regret that the US lieutenant had to be medically treated for a ruptured eardrum. I certainly had not wanted this, but where there is planning, there are also shavings. By the way, his conversation partner was lucky; he had worn his tanker helmet and had escaped powdered but unharmed.

I apologized to the American lieutenant in person. He reached out to me, and we had a laugh about the crazy scene together.

I caught his boys really on the hop, he admitted straight away.

He assured me that the last time a German soldier took a member of his family by surprise was in the Ardennes during the Battle of the Bulge.

"That could well have been my grandfather," I replied, and we both laughed heartily about it.

His superiors were, unfortunately, less conciliatory.

My superiors didn't really want to punish me; at least they said they didn't, but the NATO allies put a lot of pressure on them.

I was a hero to my comrades, but it didn't do me any good. The completion of the NATO maneuver also marked the end of my time as a Jäger.

EDEKA – End of career!

And I also had to say goodbye to my South German homeland ...

To Counter-Air Defense

Well, technically speaking, I wasn't punished.

But the transfer to the anti-aircraft troops in Cologne was undoubtedly not a reward either. Although this transfer was accompanied by promotion, it was also accompanied by a transfer to another military branch.

My new company belonged to the "Hawkies," meaning those comrades who handled the MIM-23 Hawk anti-aircraft missiles. They told me that I was supposed to help out in the Hawkies' training company as an assistant instructor for small-arms training. So basically, I did the same job, just somewhere else. My new Hawkie comrades were all right, but I was the only Swabian by far.

I missed my friends from Ludwigsburg. The greater distance to my homeland was not very helpful either. Furthermore, the linguistic distance between my Swabian dialect and the Lower Rhine language prevailing in the barracks made me believe that I was abroad.

My state of mind only improved when the company welcomed another newcomer:

Martin Schaaf, simply called "High Tower" because of his size, was a gentle giant 2.10 meters tall (that is 7.2 feet). He came from the Bavarian Forest and was an honest soul. He was as strong as a bear and blessed with a fabulous shoe size of 23, which is why the nickname "Bigfoot" was stuck on him, too.

Like me, he had been posted to Cologne because of an incident – at least that's what he told me. I could never verify the truth of the following story, but it is also too good not to be told:

Initially, Martin Schaaf had been stationed with a tank pioneer battalion in Bavaria as a tank driver, to be precise. He rode around in a recovery tank 2A1. It was always a mystery to me how a man of his height could have been chosen to drive a tank, but OK. It was usual in Bavaria at that time to have a glass of beer for lunch in the mess hall. Unfortunately, High Tower was plagued by an enormous weakness: His body could not tolerate alcohol, not a single drop. One beer was enough, and he was dead drunk. Then he ultimately got out of control and rioted such that the people near him had to immediately flee to safety. Of course, he knew this and refused alcohol like the devil avoids holy water. This was no easy undertaking in Bavaria in the late '80s. Schaaf's abstinence from alcohol regularly made his comrades mock him, culminating in a few jokers mixing schnapps into his lunchtime stew.

High Tower was literally running amok that day.

He dismantled the mess hall furnishings, then ran to the vehicle hangars and commandeered a recovery tank. He flattened first an innocent telephone booth and then the relatively new Daimler of his battalion commander.

It turned out that he had been bottled behind his back in the interrogations, which probably saved his neck. The commander now had no means of punishing him, so what did he do? He had him transferred. And High Tower ended up in the Hawkie bunch with me.

*

Now one could get the impression that the anti-aircraft troops in Cologne were designated a penalty unit. Of course, that wasn't the case. It really wrongs the comrades there. It was a coincidence that brought High Tower and me together in the Rhineland. He soon became a good friend, too.

To my knowledge, the two of us were the only soldiers in the entire Cologne barracks who came from the wild south. In any case, communication with High Tower worked much better than with the natives. Most *Nordlichts* can hardly distinguish between Bavarian and Swabian ... and *Nordlichts* for us Southern Germans are all those who live north of Württemberg and Bavaria. For the sake of simplicity, I count Franconia as one of Bavaria's exceptions. I also take Hesse out; these people are once again of a very peculiar kind. The same applies to our southern "Yellow Feet" from Baden. This somewhat idiosyncratic classification dates back to the time of the Germanic tribes when the ancestors of today's Swabians and Bavarians were regarded as the wildest and most bloodthirsty warriors. At least that's what Roman historians tell us.

The fictitious border I described between North and South Germany is also known as the *Weisswurst Equator*. Life north of this equator was different enough for us Southern Germans to think of it as a different culture. And those Northern comrades who mocked us because of our dialect didn't make us feel more at home, especially since we really tried to speak clearly and in High German ... something that we barbarians from the south really find hard to do.

I, for example, was usually banned from talking on the radio because nobody understood me except High Tower. His dialect was no different, so we joined forces. Soon he was even put in the armory with me.

Three Days of Anxiety

Service in the armory still gave me pleasure. I liked to train others and improve their skills. Soon after I settled down in Cologne, I began to toy with the idea of committing myself beyond my compulsory military service. Life as a regular soldier was something I could get enthusiastic about.

Meanwhile, the Cold War reached the final climax and achieved its (temporary?) end. First, the border to the GDR opened, and the Warsaw Pact disintegrated. Our former enemy crumbled before our eyes, and history took its course. The period between the fall of the Berlin Wall and German reunification was an exciting time for the Bundeswehr. Martin and I were initially able to take it relatively easy in the armory without knowing what was happening on the global political stage. A hot war between East and West, which is known only to a few, was entirely possible in those days, perhaps closer than ever. In any case, it was by no means a foregone conclusion that the German Democratic Republic would simply disintegrate and merge into the Federal Republic of Germany. A nervous officer in a critical position at that time would have been enough to heat up the Cold War in its final phase. Of course, buried in our armory Martin and I didn't notice anything of the hustle and bustle behind the scenes: AWACS reconnaissance aircraft patrolled the inner-German border up and down. From NATO Air Base Geilenkirchen, these sophisticated machines monitored every movement of the Warsaw Pact troops.

Even before the border's opening, the GDR's National People's Army (NVA) mobilized its elite paratroopers. It commanded them to march towards Berlin to have them up to their sleeves if necessary for suppressing demonstrations. NVA tank forces also received similar orders in those days. Alarmed by the East German troops' activities, some Russian commanders of the Soviet forces stationed on GDR soil also mobilized their troops. They probably feared a chain reaction if the East German government unleashed their soldiers on the demonstrators and wanted to be prepared for it.

On the western side, it was confirmed that Soviet units were warming up the tank engines, and the GDR elite forces were marching on Berlin. Furthermore, the increased activity on many of the Warsaw Pact's air bases had by no means escaped NATO's notice. Its fleets in the Baltic Sea and the North Sea were also suddenly very busy. So, it came about that on both sides of the border, the armed forces lying in wait came to life. Fighter-interceptors took off and monitored the airspace. Ships left their harbors and set course for the high seas.

At first, it was not clear to me whether the NATO alert that finally reached us in Cologne was an exercise or whether this time the often-threatened crisis was actually looming over the Alliance. First of all, our barracks were cut off from the outside world; all telephones, including the telephone booths, were switched off. We had to pack our personal effects in labeled boxes and hand them in. Vehicles were refueled, spare canisters filled, consumables loaded, and everything made combat-ready.

Forms for wills were issued.

We received enough food for three days and were armed and equipped with ammunition. Each soldier received 240 rounds of 7.62 mm x 51 mm NATO ammo for the G3, dispensed in filled aluminum magazines sealed watertight in foil. Whether it was an exercise or not, the ammunition I was holding in my hands at the time was live ammunition produced for the war. The aluminum magazines were not suitable for frequent use, as the magazine jaws quickly broke or bent, resulting in jams. These aluminum magazines were disposables, that's all. More stable steel magazines existed for peacetime operations.

Paradoxically, however, the troops mainly used the basically unsuitable aluminum magazines, due to the fact that ready-to-expire ammunition from the many Bundeswehr and NATO depots was constantly being issued to us; we had no way to expend it except in the aluminum magazines, and the empty magazines were then simply reused. Suitable or not!

However, this time, we had not been given superimposed ammunition whose expiration date was approaching, a circumstance that frightened me. We were all driven by silent fears. A feeling of helpless unknowing, roiled our stomachs. My fellow soldiers were silent and introverted in those days; the usual barracks life came to a complete standstill. For days we waited in our barracks-rooms, fully prepared to fight, without knowing what was going on in the outside world. When I walked through the corridors of my block, driven by boredom, at times I thought I was in church, it was so quiet – several men were squatting in every room, but none of them spoke a word. That uncanny silence even spread to the mess hall. Only the rattling of cutlery and crockery could be heard during the meals.

For three whole days, we were on pins and needles expecting at any moment the order to move out, which would have meant the beginning of the great war, West against East – and probably also the end of Europe as we knew it.

When the situation on the inner-German border finally relaxed, and it became clear that the Warsaw Pact was not planning military actions against us, the official all-clear was spread. The Russians and their allies returned to their home bases; NATO troops did the same. We were allowed to return the live ammunition, taking care that the foil into which the magazines were sealed was not damaged. In return, we got our personal effects back. The communication lines were reestablished, and we were allowed to inform our families. As a result, life in the barracks returned to usual; we soldiers did our duty as if nothing had ever happened, as if humanity had not been on the brink of what would probably have been the most immense and most terrible war in history.

My Grandpa had a Carbine!

One of the recurring tasks in the armory was belting the MG rounds, another prime example of the sometimes blatant backwardness of the Bundeswehr. We still belted the rounds like our grandfathers in Wehrmacht times, namely with a manually operated belting machine, which stuffed the cartridges into the reusable belt pockets. For hours we cranked and filled box after box with ammunition belts.

Meanwhile, the Americans and other NATO members had been using disintegrating ammo belts for a long time – they came with already belted cartridges.

Now I knew from a reliable source that the Bundeswehr had also procured such disintegrating belts but had not allowed us to use them. Unfortunately, I've never been able to find out the reason for that. Other useful accessories for our MG3 were not available in my time, either; for example, belt drums, containers for two spare barrels, and belt-insertion devices.

For other firearms, other equally useful accessories existed – just not in our armory. We requested clip-on carrying devices for the G3 rifle in vain, like the ones available on the G1 already fixed-on. Also, bipods, bayonets, and the corresponding adapters were not available either. After my time, some of these things probably eventually found their way to the troops; others, like the gun carriage which allowed the MG3 to be used as a heavy machine gun, actually even was available at our armory.

Once again, I became creative. Together with Martin and other *Kameraden*, I experimented with welded optic carriers on UZI covers or shafts for the pistol P1, unfortunately only with moderate success. We were able to obtain bayonet adapters, bayonets, and straps via private channels, mainly from Norway, Spain, Pakistan, or Turkey. These states also used the G3 or similar weapons or produced them under license themselves. HOWEVER, a G3 rifle with a bayonet mounted to it is a rather unusual sight, as the bayonet is fixed over the barrel and not beneath it.

Sometimes I could even teach High Tower a thing or two. He was able to handle firearms well, but he lacked the theoretical foundation. He once asked me to hand him the carbine from the workbench while cleaning up the armory. However, on the workbench, I only saw an extensively-damaged G3 rifle that had not been helped by the recruits' cleaning efforts.

"What carbine?" I asked. "There's just an old G3, isn't there?"

"Yes, that's exactly what I mean, man!" Martin replied, annoyed.

"Jesus Christ, how many times do I have to explain this to you!" I answered angrily. "My blessed grandpa had a carbine with him in Russia, a Mauser K98k, to be exact! You'll have to have your old coati ass get transferred to the *Wachbataillon* if you want to see a carbine in the Bundeswehr!"

*

From time to time, we even got to see extraordinary things in Cologne. Once I was given the opportunity to see a prototype of the new super assault rifle G11 from Heckler & Koch in action.

This weapon used a groundbreaking technique that utilized caseless ammunition. The designers of the G11 did without the classic cocking lever – instead, a rotary switch was attached to the weapon. The huge 45-shot magazine resembled a carpenter's level in its design and was mounted above the barrel. The 4.73-mm x 33-mm caliber cartridges were ignited electrically. A reflector sight allowed for precise aiming. The G11 reached 500 rounds per minute in a continuous fire; even the legendary (theoretical) output of 2000 rounds per minute was thinkable using three-shot fire bursts.

It was precisely machined and easy to handle.

Unfortunately, I was only allowed to look at it from a distance, not touch it myself. As is generally known, the G11 never went into production, but at some point, disappeared into the archives of Heckler & Koch. I was facing the same fate (of course, I wasn't supposed to be stored in the archives of H&K, but like the G11, I simply wasn't allowed to stay with the troops).

*

During my time in Cologne, the camouflage uniform still in use today was gradually introduced. We wore our good old stone-grey-olive moleskin clothes, which were already a considerable improvement compared to the felt-material battle dress my father had to wear during his time in the *Bund*. But the new camouflage uniforms were another class better; we were convinced of that.

First, the combat units like the paratroopers and the Jägers received the new uniforms.

We, on the other hand, had to use up all the old models first.

But there was a sergeant in Cologne, who had been a paratrooper before and who passed the legendary German commando course. He was one tough guy. He didn't have much service time left before returning to civilian life, so he was attached to the maintenance unit. But even there, he paraded his front-line pig capabilities and probably would have preferred to march into Moscow alone.

This guy was the real deal.

No one knows how he did it, but he had gotten hold of some new camouflage print bolts and now forced his poor wife to sew him a combat uniform out of it. The result, of course, did not look as professional as the commercially made uniforms but did not prevent him from wearing the self-made thing all day long. He became the laughingstock of the whole barracks, much to his displeasure.

*

On another occasion, I watched a whole platoon of soldiers marching from morning to night through a long and very shallow basin of water to test the new combat boots that the manufacturer promised would keep water out for seven hours. Judging by the long faces, the footgear didn't deliver what it promised. In any case, the boots were a permanent topic among us soldiers. Many were dissatisfied with what the Bundeswehr made available and therefore bought other models privately.

Civilians Meet Soldiers

More out of boredom, but also out of necessity, I registered for a military car-driving license. My civil license was not valid for the Bundeswehr – and the fact that I already had a military truck license in my pocket did not count either.

When I received the permit to attend the driving course, it was already winter. I took my lessons with a VW Iltis in the snow. For those of you who don't know: It's not a pleasure! And my driving instructor also turned out to be a psychopath. I still wonder how this guy got into the sergeant ranks. A thick, stinking cigar was constantly stuck between his teeth, and he liked to blow the smoke around my ears during a drive.

Once, when it was snowing heavily, he suddenly told me to pull over. He turned to me and asked with a stern look: "How fast were you going?"

I answered truthfully: "50 kilometers per hour."

"And what was on the last traffic sign?" he asked inscrutably.

"I don't know; it was all snowed over," I replied.

"Then get out now, walk the 400 meters back to the sign, wipe away the snow and read what it says!"

It was like that all along. I think you call it "harassment."

On another occasion, he had me and another student driver, who had an outstanding gap between his incisors, stop on the shoulder of the autobahn. He actually wanted us to search the grassy area behind the guardrail in the pouring rain for a windscreen wiper that had just flown off! My comrade with the gap between his teeth complained because this wet idea meant danger to life and limb – the autobahn was full of cars driving 150 kilometers per hour and more – but our psycho teacher probably thought we just wouldn't want to go out into the rain.

"No tooth in your snout, but wanna whistle La Paloma and then howl because of a little water! This way, you'll never get your name on a war memorial," he bellowed and insisted that we take up the search. After a two-hour hunt for the lost wiper, during which it rained pitchforks without interruption, we actually found the missing part – far away from the crash barrier in a ditch. We were soaked to the bone, frozen, and caught a cold. The windshield wiper was, of course, fodder for the trash can.

Somehow the golden soldier's rule of never volunteering for anything made sense to me again ...

*

When civilians meet uniforms, strange things happen. A curious event occurred on an otherwise typical day. We were in the armory doing maintenance when the phone rang. I answered the call. Our CO, Lieutenant Siebert, told me: "Schober, we need ... um ... a few volunteers to bring back some of our lambs that must have gotten lost. I was thinking of you!"

Silence on the phone line.

After an eternity, I replied: "Of me?"

"Yes, Schober. I know the military police usually do that. Still, they're all on their way to secure an event with important characters from Bonn. And the military police at the gate can't leave their post."

"And what shall I do?" I asked.

"Grab another man, preferably this Schaaf guy, and pick up a vehicle from the motor pool. I've already told them you're coming. Then you'll drive to the main gate. I'll leave all the papers and a map with the guard there."

"Uh ... yes ... yes, *Herr Leutnant*. What's going on?"

"The Cologne police called. They received some calls from panicked civilians who have seen armed soldiers wandering through their neighborhood. We have some squads on orientation marches on the move, you know. Maybe somebody's got lost.

"Your mission: get to the agreed meeting point with the police patrol, coordinate with them, then start a joint search for the soldiers roaming around. Collect them and return them. Report back to me!"

"Uh ... Yes, copy that." This was followed, of course, by me repeating the order, as every decent soldier was conditioned into doing: "Drive to the agreed meeting point with police patrol, meet them, then search for the soldiers roaming around together. Collect and return them, report back to you."

"Do it!" the lieutenant's voice boomed.

"Yes, *Herr Leutnant!*" I replied reflexively, then I hung up and called out to High Tower: "Let's go, Martin, we have an order from the boss. Excursion with a scavenger hunt!"

The motor pool still had a rickety VW bus, whose paint was streaked with rust stains and whose shock absorbers were heavily damaged.

The private on duty grinned at us.

Sighing, I signed the papers, and together with High Tower in the old rattletrap, I set off for the main gate. When we arrived there, one of the MP guards handed us a stack of papers, including a map and directions to the meeting point with the police. We found it relatively quickly, contacted the two officers waiting there, and then continued on together. High Tower climbed into the patrol car, and I took one of the policemen with me in the VW bus.

First, we drove to an address where we spoke to an elderly lady who had called the police. Obviously, the soldiers, armed to the teeth, were on their way to the local railway station; at least that's what we learned from what the frightened woman told us. We talked it over briefly and decided to go directly to the station.

On the way, we saw nothing conspicuous. Arriving at the station, however, our eyes were offered a genuinely cinematic scene: *Darth Vader* and a delegation of his stormtroopers, in full dress and equipped with science fiction weapons, marched towards the main entrance of the local station.

Turns out there was a *Star Wars* convention that day. Some foreign fans had caught the wrong train and had happened to land in the suburb near the barracks. They had been wandering around looking for the convention venue before deciding to return to the station. The unaware residents – especially the older ones – had probably mistaken the costumed people for invasion forces of a foreign power. The Star Wars fans finally found their convention, with the friendly support of the local police. Later I heard that this misunderstanding was repeated several times in the following years.

*

Encounters between civilians and soldiers could also be less pleasant like I experienced more and more since my transfer to Cologne.

I was able to walk home from the Ludwigsburg barracks on Friday afternoons. Now I had to use public transport to get from Cologne via Stuttgart to my hometown. If no one in Ludwigsburg had been bothered when I wandered around in my uniform and my duffel bag filled with dirty laundry – Ludwigsburg is an old garrison town where soldiers were on the road at all times – on the bus and train journey from Cologne to Stuttgart, I was constantly mobbed and spat at.

"You're all potential murderers!" were the emotional cries that some citizens threw at us. Basically, you could only go home in civilian clothes. A lot of Bundeswehr units even recommended this in the first place.

However, older people usually had nice words for us. They had often experienced a war themselves and therefore appreciated our contribution to the preservation of peace.

In one case, a grandmother even protected me from a haranguing student and attacked her with her walking stick. The completely amazed student and her friends then took flight.

But since my transfer, I preferred to travel in civilian clothes.

Of course, we conscripts were recognized immediately by our duffel bags and short hairstyle. I also quickly realized that I always met the same guys on Friday afternoons and Sunday evenings on the train platforms.

I remember one of them particularly well.

We called him the "Sausage Slider."

On Sunday evenings, he always had sandwiches with him, which his mother must have prepared for him, and which he ate on the train to Cologne as a real treat.

That wouldn't be anything special in itself. However, the way he did this was unique: First, he ate the sausage from the bread until only a tiny slice was left. But now he had a big slice of bread with only a tiny slice of sausage on it. So, he pushed the last piece of sausage back and forth on the bread and bit only a small edge of the slice of sausage but at the same time a large piece of bread. Hence his name: Sausage Slider.

As long as I was on the same route as him, he didn't deviate from this ritual.

*

By the way, I also remember later on when members of the federal parliament and other officials from the Social Democratic and the Green political spectrum. At the time of my military service, they demonstrated unilateral disarmament of the West and against nuclear weapons, including protests in front of the gate of my military home base. Some protesters insulted us conscripts when we went to the barracks or wanted to leave them. Still, technically we were not even voluntarily in the armed forces. The protesters' colorful banners, posters, and the transfigured slogans on them are still fixed in my memory.

I wonder what would have happened if the demands of the peace movement had been fully met. How would the politicians of these days get German citizens out of crisis regions such as Libya in 2011 (Operation Pegasus) or participate in international peace missions in the Mediterranean Basin or Africa? Who would fish refugees from the Mediterranean or put pirates in their place on the

Horn of Africa? For some politicians, at any rate, the following seems to apply: "What do I care about my gossip and my actions of yesterday?"

With their later approval of the Afghanistan war, some of our former peace apostles even sent the Bundeswehr into a combat zone to "defend Germany at the Hindu Kush" and are thus jointly responsible for more than 50 fallen German soldiers. Who will ask this year about the bereaved and the friends of the fallen, of whom I am also one? Why does our society hardly ever cultivate public remembrance of the fallen of the Federal Republic of Germany?

These are our friends, brothers, fathers.

Why are those who have made the greatest sacrifice not honored? A hidden memorial on the Ministry of Defense's grounds in Berlin must apparently suffice for those who want to honor their memory.

It's not enough for me!

In general, I am often disturbed by our Berlin politics. As a former soldier, interested reservist, and enthusiastic marksman, I often get to know the absurdities of the prevailing conditions firsthand. For me, the German weapons laws already mentioned above are a prime example of a misguided policy driven by blind politicking. After regaining its national sovereignty, the then still-young Federal Republic had adopted the National Socialists' weapons laws almost without hesitation. Under the rule of that well-known Austrian corporal, these very laws were initiated to block access to weapons for unwanted population groups and political opponents. Only party members and patrons of the Nazis were allowed to continue to arm themselves. This way, their dominance was assured!

In the further course of time, the various German postwar history incidents have repeatedly been seized as the opportunity to tighten the weapons laws even further, according to the motto: "We are doing something!"

The only problem was that what was done did not even affect those intended to deter – namely, the criminals who were not interested in any weapons laws anyway. This was deliberately concealed. Often, politics and the press acted as two mutually supportive players, and I observe that they still do.

Needless to say, the Red Army Fraction terrorists had not applied for a gun license before committing their murders and armed robberies. Other terrorists and gangsters also procure their pieces illegally. Nevertheless, after sensational acts by criminals, every time, the German weapons laws were tightened up.

And crimes with weapons will continue to be committed in the future, no matter how strict German or European laws may become. It only affects those who are not guilty of anything anyway: The sport shooters, the hunters, the collectors.

Only once such institutions have entirely disappeared – because the hunter, for example, will no longer be able to afford the proper locking-up and carrying his rifle due to ever more bureaucratic hurdles, combined with ever-higher costs – will society notice what it has lost.

What's the unintended loss?

"Only when the last car is scrapped, and the last gas station is closed will you notice that Greenpeace does not sell beer at night."

I would welcome it if ordinary citizens were to question these things more critically.

Sergeant JA

We conscripts were happy to have every opportunity to earn some extra money. The Bundeswehr pay wasn't very generous, after all. And there were such possibilities for earning that extra money, you just had to know-how! In Cologne, the flow of NATO personnel was enormous – many came to exercises on a daily or weekly basis or were passing through. Of course, these people were keen on souvenirs from Germany! Badges had always been exchanged by soldiers with pleasure. The US-Americans, above all, were wild about German cuckoo clocks. Now, many *Ami's* have a completely wrong picture of us – believe we drink only beer, eat only potatoes and bratwurst with sauerkraut and black bread, live in castles or half-timbered houses, and wear leather pants and dirndls all day long. One Ami was stunned by the skyscrapers towered up into the sky from downtown Cologne and by the motorways that crisscrossed North Rhine-Westphalia. He had not expected such achievements of civilization in Germany. Another American wanted to know from High Tower whether we still tortured our captured enemies. We looked at each other, grinning. Martin answered that we would sharpen pencils to push them under the fingernails of prisoners. He said it so seriously, the Yank went chalk pale. Of course, we straightened him out afterward.

Anyway, the Americans, in particular, were pleased to spend money on souvenirs ... so why not? We conscripts got the desired things at Cologne military-surplus dealers and from mail-order sellers: badges of all the Bundeswehr units, beer mugs, and – of course – cuckoo clocks.

Then we sold the things (with a small surcharge) to Americans, British and other allies who found their way to Cologne. Often, we also exchanged stuff. My camping equipment came together in this way: US boots, French cooker, British sleeping bag, Belgian tent ... and everything packed in a beautiful aluminum air transport box from the Netherlands. Very helpful in all the business was my temporary love relationship with a US Air Force sergeant. That may sound strange at first, but no, I'm not queer at all! Sergeant Joyce Alberta McKenna was one hell of a tough woman.

I jokingly called her "Sergeant JA."

She would have casually defeated most of the men I know in arm wrestling and am a real musclewoman. I never really liked this kind of dame, but Sergeant JA was someone exceptional. Our first encounter took place on the shooting range. She fired an American M60 machine gun in a standing shoulder position, not the usual hip position. That was difficult for many men. For a woman, it was an incredible show. She also hit the targets pretty well!

I wouldn't have been able to do anything comparable with our MG3.

It must be said that women in uniform were a rare sight for German soldiers of the years 1989 and 1990. Only the medical and military band service was open to the female sex at that time; otherwise, only men cavorted in the Bundeswehr barracks. Some people did not see a single uniformed woman during their military service, so our interest in any ladies in uniform was all the greater. With the Americans (and the Dutch), it was already different at that time. The Russians had pure women's regiments during the Second World War, and their snipers were feared by the Germans. The Israelis have also had good experiences with women in the armed forces. However, their women are only allowed to serve in training and auxiliary troops, not in combat units.

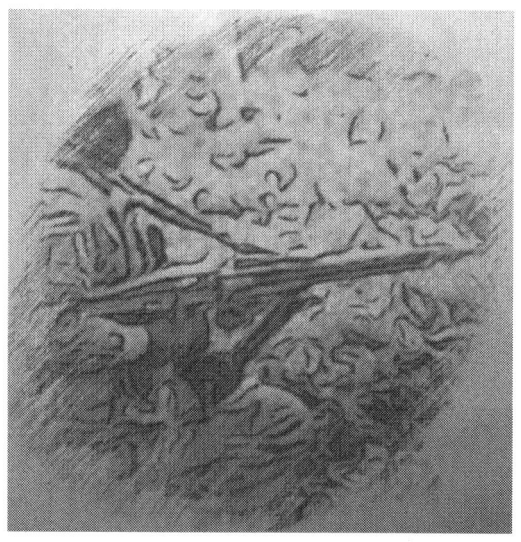

Incidentally, the Americans have found in a series of experiments that tank crews of either men-only or women-only work more efficiently on the battlefield than mixed-sex crews. In mixed crews, when a female crew member was wounded, all the men immediately took care of her, leading to general inattention and thus often to failure. I'll just leave it at that.

In any case, I do not know whether the Americans are actively taking these findings into account. At any rate, I have never even come across a mixed US tank crew.

But back to Sergeant JA. Apart from the obvious charms, I was particularly impressed by her skills in handling weapons that day on the shooting range.

I just had to get to know that woman!

A little later, I got my chance in another match with the Americans. The allies were allowed to try out our irons, and we were allowed to try theirs. With the right timing and a bit of help from High Tower, who set the order for the shooting, Sergeant JA ended up behind the MG I watched over as shooting supervisor.

Nothing like good friends in the right place!

We spent our time chatting, united by our interest in weapons and militaria. We continued our conversation at every break. When the shooting ended, I gathered all my courage and invited her to dinner. One thing led to another, and in the end, we were together for six incredible months. From this point on – I gladly admit this – my homesickness was very limited. I didn't get back to Ludwigsburg that much anymore, either.

A nice side-effect of my relationship with Joyce was the access to the PX, a shop for members of the US-services exclusively, which offered a lot of goods that you couldn't get by other means at that time. I remember hauling tons of root beer, barbecue sauces, and thick T-bone steaks out of the store. In my family and circle of acquaintances, I always found enough buyers for surplus purchases.

I was especially keen on a pair of Fort Lewis Boots and a real KA-BAR combat knife. The boots were costly, a sinful 499 Deutsche Marks (about 300 US Dollars at that time), and outside the PX, they were just not available. Fort Lewis is like the Ferrari of fighting boots.

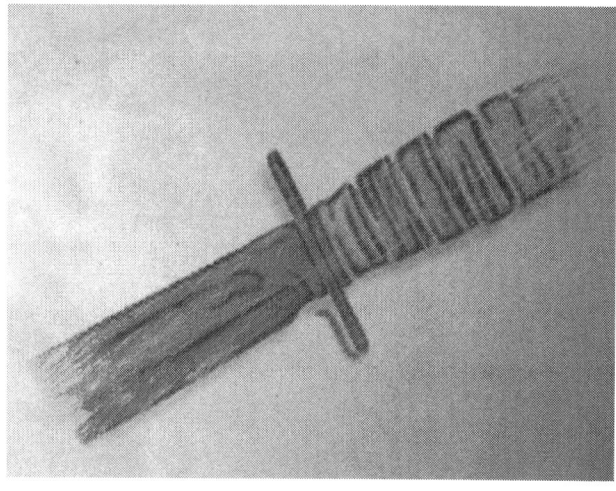

When I asked about sizes available, with a twinkle in his eye, the salesman told me that he was not selling children's coffins. Well, was he lucky that High Tower didn't come to see him! I was holding a pair my size in my hands after a week for delivery.

Through Joyce, I got to know many Americans better; mostly, they had landed in Cologne while visiting troops or passing through, and then – with the warmest recommendation of my girlfriend – came to me to stock up on souvenirs. What High Tower and I were doing there already bordered on an honest merchant's business, and we can only be glad that neither the tax office nor the operator of the enlisted men's club got wind of the matter.

*

Two months before my duty time ended, Joyce was transferred back to the States. She gave me her Air Force KA-BAR combat knife, which I still cherish.

Unfortunately, I never saw her again.

Plan B

High Tower and I had finally concluded that we should try to sign up for another tour and later perhaps even become professional soldiers. Unfortunately, the downfall of the Warsaw Pact thwarted our pious plans. Four weeks before the end of our military service, our CO and the *Spiess* had certified to the personnel department that we would commit ourselves as regular soldiers.

The papers weren't signed yet. And we poor compatriots had no idea why those papers were so long in coming. So, we sat together and planned our future in the *Bund*, raved about training courses all over the country, and dreamed of eventually ascending to the position of NCO.

One Monday morning, two weeks before my end of duty, everything changed. The entire company had to line up outside the block.

"Company, stand to attention! – For reporting to the commanding officer, eeeeeyes – left!"

Our CO was standing in front of us, downcast, reading an order that all conscripts were to muster out of the unit prematurely.

That, of course, applied to High Tower, and me too!

The reason for this was that there was suddenly no need for regular soldiers anymore since the plan was to integrate at least some of the soldiers from the NVA. At the same time, Germany had obliged itself to reduce its overall troop strength.

So that's it with our plan A.

EDEKA time (end of career)!

So, I was allowed correspondingly to return home two weeks early, making up 18 months of military service minus two weeks. Our time was up. Over and done.

That's how Martin and I parted ways.

Epilogue

In the end, my thoughts come back to that bar. Crouching on the cold tiles, High Tower, two Hawkies, and I tried frantically to hold the table over our heads, our only cover. Around us, loaded Americans and British beat each other up – for some stupid and completely unimportant reason. Bottles flew, burst on the floor, splinters swirled over the tiles. Blood flowed everywhere.

Shortly afterward, the US military police arrived on the scene. As usual, our German MPs didn't show up for such tussles.

The military policemen from overseas, grim characters whose bull necks swelled out of their collars and whose arms full of muscles reminded me of tree trunks, backed an army truck up to the entrance. At the same time, a second task force blocked the rear exit. A rapid-engagement force was formed at lightning speed; the MP's, reminiscent of gorillas, finally stormed the pub. Armed with white truncheons, they mercilessly plowed through the crowd of combatants. The noise took on grotesque features; men screamed sharply under the blows of the truncheons. British and Americans went down. In a dark corner, a Yank slept out his intoxication, hanging crookedly in his chair; unimpaired by the tumult, he snored so loudly that he even drowned out the noise of the fight. He might tip over at any moment. At least that's what it looked like.

Meanwhile, the MP's battered the drunkards with mechanical precision. Again and again, the white impact weapons rose from heads, uniforms, and fists' tangle and disappeared into them again. Dull thuds followed, and the groaning of those who were hit by blows pressed the air out of their lungs. The drunks went down whimpering, one by one. The military policemen knew their business. They weren't doing it for the first time and obviously enjoyed their job. The writhing and the sleeping were grabbed by the second wave of policemen and tossed into the truck's cargo area with little squeamishness. Slowly, the well-smashed pub was emptied; the noise gave way to the commands, and the MP troop's boot kicks, functioning like clockwork. We were still sitting under the table. High-proof swill, tobacco, and sweat formed the basis for a sweetish-sharp taint in the air.

Finally, two giants of military policemen arrived at our table. With their shovel-like hands, they reached for us and dragged us roughly from under our cover. We wore civilian clothes and were not immediately recognizable as Germans. I saw the threateningly raised truncheons, my arms reflexively up in front of my face. The pub's innkeeper, who knew us well, jumped to our aid. He tried to clarify the situation. He had probably called the military police in the first place for fear that the drunken stiffs would tear the entire place apart. Even so, the damage done was immense, as could be seen at a glance.

The innkeeper and the American military policemen exchanged a few words, using a mixture of English and German. Nevertheless, our dear comrades from America let themselves be dissuaded from their plan to bag us. We breathed a sigh of relief.

Unfortunately, again and again, soldiers of different nationalities rioted in the Cologne area. The density of military installations there was very high at that time, and countless pubs fueled the alcohol consumption of young men, and it was the only pastime for many.

The pub where we had witnessed the clobbering was an important meeting point for us, Hawkies. Less than 100 meters away from the barracks gate, it had quickly become a favorite place for us to kill time. The innkeeper, an honest Cologne fellow, always had an open ear for our young troopers' worries. He also knew the problems of High Tower in connection with alcohol. He, therefore, kept a gimlet eye out so that only children's drinks were served to him.

That pub was simply a place where we felt at home, where we also spent countless hours. I still feel melancholic today when I think back to the conversations I had with my comrades there about everybody and his dog, between blue haze and blond beers. Together we flirted, argued, sang ... even cried. The innkeeper's wife, who came from Böblingen in Baden-Württemberg and had therefore added dishes from that region on the menu, always gave me a little bit of home in faraway Cologne. Her dialect alone reminded me of home, and I always enjoyed talking to her. Their homemade Swabian pockets in broth, *Schupfnudels* with pointed cabbage, and hand-scraped spaetzle with sauce were pure poetry!

I miss those days of lightheartedness.

The weisswurst eating contest, regularly celebrated in the pub, also made High Tower happy, so there was something for everyone. Shortly before our end of duty, we visited the pub one last time to say goodbye to the innkeeper, his kindhearted wife, and the pretty blonde waitress Marie.

It was our last evening together in Cologne.

The next morning, the first of us were released into civilian life, including High Tower. Shortly after that, my service also ended. Thus, a wonderful time, of which I will have fond memories all my life, came to an end for me.

Martin and I stayed in touch, but I only saw him again at his funeral. I almost didn't recognize him anymore; cancer had disfigured him so. It's awful how degenerate cells, only visible under a microscope, can force a giant like Martin to his knees.

Despite the circumstances, my buddy Frank managed to become a regular soldier, made it a career. He was killed on his second mission in Afghanistan.

I miss him very much.

I didn't see Tasso and Paul again.

Today Bankwat is an alternative-medicine practitioner and also offers Thai massages.

Peter took over his parents' farm.

I started a job as an electrician in the mechanical engineering industry.

But in my heart, I have always remained a Jäger.

I had to live my plan B! But plan B sucks. Otherwise, it'd be plan A, wouldn't it? What did Yogi Berra once say?

"If the world was perfect, it wouldn't be."

Hindsight

Since its foundation in the 1950s, conscripts and temporary and professional soldiers of the Bundeswehr have been ready to function as the shield and sword of the Federal Republic of Germany. They were the shield that protected the people of Western democracies from the communist threat posed by the Warsaw Pact; at least, that's what the leaders and politicians of the so-called Free World long made clear to their voters. For many decades, armies that were in place and always more or less ready to fight faced each other on the border that divided Europe into East and West. If the Warsaw Pact had committed its colossal forces, the soldiers on both sides would have been faced with certain death if an armed conflict had actually taken place on Central European soil. Germany willingly included its territory as a potential battlefield in NATO's emergency plans. These plans ultimately provided for the widespread use of nuclear weapons on the soil of the Federal Republic of Germany in order to effectively stop attacking enemy forces and create an almost impassable killing zone in the center of Europe.

These are historical facts.

We can all be glad that such simulation-games have never left the drawers of NATO strategists and that we have been spared a third world war to this day. But it is also a fact that the people in uniform at that time, soldiers, were willing to give their lives for that of their fellow citizens – for the common good of all Germans and Europeans, and in the face of every threat. The protesters and rioters, who insulted these soldiers as murderers and warmongers and demonstrated against the military in general, benefited from this protection, which also secured their freedom of speech and right to demonstrate. It is precisely these freedoms that were protected by the members of the Bundeswehr, mostly unnoticed by the public and at the risk of their own lives and physical integrity.

The Bundeswehr has always been its own world, understandable only to those who have served and who thus recognize its value to society. For many young men, military service was part of an average career for decades, as was the fact that during military service, they met people they would never have met without the Bundeswehr. Such accidental interpersonal contacts within the generation of young adults are likely to have decreased significantly since the abolition of conscription. Unfortunately, this also means that social insights into other classes of society and their living conditions get lost. We, Tom Zola, and I fear that this will mean that many fellow citizens will never look beyond their own sphere of existence and will thus remain closed to the reality of the lives of others. Understanding for fellow human beings shrinks, thereby leading to a growing fissure of our society. Today there is much talk of parallel societies, and we are in the process of expanding and cementing them. A student will hardly talk to a journeyman, a commercial employee, or a bank clerk to a nurse or motor mechanic. They just rarely meet in our society today.

Such encounters were and still are the order of the day in the Bundeswehr, making it a unique organization. Today, many young people lack the discipline, independence, and self-confidence that can be acquired through military service. The camaraderie and the often lifelong friendships made in the Bundeswehr are also denied to many today.

Otherwise, we, Hartmut Schober and Tom Zola, the authors of this book, only have to repeat what Tom, together with our fellow author Stefan Köhler, have already summed up in their book "Einsatzbericht: Krieg in Afghanistan":

Driven by the march of time, by changing threats in Germany and the world, by scandals of various natures, by the struggle over the relative morality of Wehrmacht-succession versus conscious new beginnings, by billions in armament failures and austerity measures, by foreign deployments; by war, which politics does not want to call war, the Bundeswehr usually is brought into public focus when there is something negative to report about it; when soldiers are killed in action when expensive armament projects fail when individuals overshadow the achievements of the great majority through extraordinary misconduct.

During the Cold War, German soldiers were regarded as solid allies who would fight even in dicey situations. What about today? Scrimping on money, with inadequate equipment and run by politics, the Bundeswehr is at best only a dubious ally for its military partners – but this is by no means the fault of our soldiers, who still accept many privations to serve their country. Instead, the blame lies with the politicians who are no longer prepared to take a clear position, who use the Bundeswehr as a bargaining chip in their own sick craving for validation, who are only anxious to advance their own prestige projects, and who have neither understanding nor a concrete idea of what it is like to serve in the military.

That the German armed forces in Afghanistan cannot carry out their own Medevac operations (rescue of wounded by helicopter) ... forget about it! That half of the battle tanks and almost the entire helicopter, combat, and transport aircraft fleet are immobile ... so what? The most important thing is that someone has finally taken on the critical subject of the maternity uniform for pregnant female soldiers, isn't it? This will solve the real problems of our armed forces! In any case, we ask ourselves how many female soldiers are affected at all – according to Tom's experience from his time on duty, most pregnant soldiers are banned from work by the doctor anyway – and rightly so.

In any case, the current state of the Bundeswehr makes us sad. Simultaneously, the Bundeswehr could inculcate discipline, self-confidence, and prudence in young people and support them in their search for meaning in their lives. All this is possible but is not taken up by our politicians. It remains to be seen whether the voters will force a change of direction.

For us, it is of crucial importance that the Bundeswehr should again rise to the status of military power of relevance. This concern is all the more important in our time when the old allies are becoming increasingly fickle. Our society, especially our young citizens, would certainly not be harmed by introducing compulsory military service for all (!) adolescents over the age of 18. A civilian service to be introduced at the same time as an alternative would do the shaken care system good and enable contact with other areas of life and provide the same positive effects as military service. The daily service in the Bundeswehr remains a mystery for large parts of the population; unfortunately, nothing can be changed in the short term, but one should finally be able to discuss the problems openly and address them without being portrayed reflexively as a warmonger.

About the Authors

Hartmut Schober, born in 1971, was drafted into the Bundeswehr – back then, the armed forces of only Western Germany – during the final phase of the Cold War. He served as a Jäger (infantryman) and later in a MIM-23 Hawk unit. As a young soldier, he witnessed the incredible tension of that historical moment when the Eastern Bloc fell apart. The Western Bloc did not know if this would mean war or peace.

After his military service, Schober worked in the munitions industry. In his free time, he does sporting marksmanship and private deer hunting. He is obsessed with weapons, military engineering, and history.

Besides being an author, Schober supports EK-2 Publishing as a military expert.

Tom Zola, a former sergeant in the German Army, is a military fiction writer famous for his intense battle descriptions and realistic action scenes. In 2014 the first book of his PANZERS series was released in the German language, setting up an alternate history scenario. A different German Reich tries to turn around the fortunes of war at the pinnacle of the Second World War. Zola doesn't beat around the bush; his stories involve brutal fighting, inhuman ideologies, and a military machine that overruns Europe and the whole world without mercy. He has developed a breathtaking yet shocking alternate timeline that has finally been translated into English.

Zola, born in 1988, is married and lives with his wife and two kids in Duisburg, Germany.

Short Story: Dance of the Bayonets
By Hartmut Schober

The thunder of the artillery shelling makes the ground tremble. A wall of fire rolls toward the enemy positions, preparing for the assault. The men stand in long lines, ready to move out of the trench into battle. There is a loud cry: "Bayonets!".

Each soldier's hand gropingly grips his hip, seeking the hilt of the blade whose scabbard hangs from his belt. At the call of "Fix bayonets!" dozens of hands pull the blade from its scabbard and attach it to the tip of the rifle with a fluid motion. The metallic sound as countless bayonet grips lock into the mount beneath the barrel ripples through the trenches like a wave spreading through an inland channel. At the command, "Prepare for attack!" the men climb narrow ladders over the breastworks, out onto the battlefield, crossing their own barbed wire entanglements in the created aisles and unfolding their formation into a broad, staggered skirmish line. Still crouched low, on one knee, holding out their rifle at the ready, they awaited the order to attack. Now the roar of the guns died down, and silence fell on the field of death. Already the call resounds: "Up, up, to the attack!".

The rifle pressed tightly in front of the chest, it goes at a brisk pace towards the enemy's trenches.

The pace gets faster with every meter. Now the men run in the uneven terrain, convulsively trying to stay in formation. Then, as if of their own accord, the weapons are lowered for the assault, towards the enemy, and a thousand throats roar their war cries. The enemy, stunned by the shelling, recognizes the danger and forms up for defense. The first fall, but the assault continues unabated. The breath goes gasping, the weapon lies heavily in the hands, but further, it goes into the hell mouth of the battle. Already the wild attack reaches the enemy's positions, overcomes the barriers, puts the opponents in their lair. The resistance is fierce but full of verve, the soldiers rush forward. Bright steel flashes as the blades cross and the man-on-man battle begins. A lunge, a thrust, the blade twisted in the flesh to enlarge the wound and prevent it from lodging in the enemy's body; a step back, withdrawing the rifle with the bayonet, and the enemy was freed from life. Only a quick sideways step avoids the hit of another enemy, parried with the butt of his own rifle, a slight turn, and a blow with the steel-shod stock of the soldier's bride, and this enemy also goes down. A searing pain suddenly pierces the left arm, a blow hits the steel helmet heavily on the side; dazed to the ground, the vision wavers. Lying on his back, at the mercy of the onslaught of an approaching adversary, who, with a face consumed by hatred, rushes wildly slavering, the rifle with the long spike bayonet raised for a deadly thrust. The eyes widened in horror, searching for his own rifle with his healthy right arm, snatching it at the last moment and stretching it towards the bloodthirsty onrushing demon. The enemy can no longer cancel his move and impales himself.

The battle is dying down, the fight is won, the enemy surrenders, but blood covers the ground of the field of honor that has been so dearly bought with the bare blade of bayonets. Soon there will be another bloody battle, and again it will be paid with the lives of so many brave soldiers in this dance of the bayonets.

Short Story: Shadow of Memory
By Hartmut Schober

Thomas thought of his wife Susanne and his two daughters as he watched the hustle and bustle on Kabul's streets, lost in thought. The dust on the Bundeswehr bus windows only allowed a veiled view, but that didn't matter; on the way home, nothing matters anyway. His friend Wolfgang, who was sitting next to him, was as usual showing off his dopey permanent grin, which had not disappeared even after several months in Afghanistan. They had already left the camp for the airfield at 7:45 a.m. on that Saturday morning with their convoy – at the head a Wolf unarmored all-terrain vehicle as an escort, then a bus loaded with luggage, the second bus with the returnees of the reconnaissance battalion from Frankenberg, a Dutch truck with more luggage and at the end of the convoy another Wolf. There was little traffic on Route *Violet* near the German *Camp Warehouse* on Saturday. The convoy made good progress but had to stop briefly at *Spaghetti Camp* to let more military vehicles turn onto the road as the Italians' camp was called in troop jargon. Already the convoy was also heading for the airport. Then suddenly, a white and yellow cab approached the convoy and tried to overtake the second bus, first on the right, then on the left. Finally, the cab pulled up next to the crowded bus, and within an instant, a vast bang tore through the traffic's background noise.

The bright flash of a detonation flickered, thousands of shards from bursting windows and shrapnel from debris flew through the air. The blast wave from the suicide bomber's 150-pound bomb hidden in the cab hurled the bus away like a child's toy. Blood, debris, and the wounded's shrill cries were everywhere, and grinning Afghans stood at the side of the road, laughing at the foreign soldiers for their carelessness and stupidity. Uninjured and lightly wounded soldiers tried to extricate their comrades from the rubble. The men sitting on the left side of the second bus had fared the worst. At some point, NATO troops arrived to assist. Allied soldiers secured the area of the attack on all sides. Afghan police dispersed the feuding crowd, and Dutch medics began treating victims. They could not help two German soldiers, their bloodied and shattered bodies held together only by their bulletproof vests. Others were so severely wounded that they died a short time later. Additional forces arrived and began providing emergency care to the wounded before evacuating them. Thomas still got to see helicopters land to fly out the wounded. A CH-53 flew over the area, then it went black around him.

When Thomas' gaze cleared, he felt the warm, soft hand of his wife Susanne tenderly squeezing his. He arrived fully back in the present and realized that he had once again been lost in his memories.

Here in the Forest of Remembrance, this happened significantly often. Since the opening in 2014, they had been here several times to remember their fallen comrades; and especially to pay their respects to their friend Wolfgang, who had once introduced them to each other and had not survived the day of the attack in 2003. Thomas and Susanne had also visited the memorial of the Bundeswehr, which had been inaugurated in 2009 on the

Ministry of Defense's grounds at the Bendlerblock in Berlin. There were usually very few people there, as the site was centrally located but off the beaten track. The building, which was undoubtedly architecturally sophisticated, consisted of a concrete cuboid 41 meters long, 8 meters wide, 10 meters high, open to the public, and a bronze shell intended to commemorate the German soldier's dog tags. Unfortunately, however, it had little of an inviting appearance – inside or out. Inside was a black room of silence. A video installation projected the names of the fallen for five seconds each. An inscription on the wall read, "To the dead of our Bundeswehr for peace, justice, and freedom."

Everything was very dark, gloomy, and cold. It reminded both Thomas and Susanne of a crypt – not a place for fond memories of friends and comrades. The Forest of Remembrance was better suited to cherish the memory and pay tribute to the fallen comrades. It was initially intended to house only the honorary groves from the respective areas of deployment. Still, it soon became a focal point for the actively lived grief of many relatives, comrades, and friends of fallen soldiers. Unfortunately, this contemplation place was also very remotely located in a wooded area near the Henning-von-Treschkow barracks in Geltow, so that many mourners shunned the long journey. One was often alone here with oneself and one's memories. Acquaintances and friends of the couple, whom they had told about their visits there, were amazed that such a place existed at all. Even the memorial of the German Armed Forces in Berlin was known to very few people – mostly only to those directly affected by a loss.

Thomas wiped a tear from his eye and turned to his wife. She had always supported him and was a great help to him even now. For nothing was he so grateful to Wolfgang as for his acquaintance with Susanne. Wolfgang had also been the godfather of their oldest daughter Marie and, after Thomas, probably the proudest man at her birth. Thomas and Susanne agreed to tell Marie about her godfather as often as they could.

For someone is truly dead only when he has been forgotten.

Short Story: My old Friend and Comrade
By Hartmut Schober

My old friend is close to me; I feel his coming.
All my life, he was a faithful companion.
Wherever I went, wherever life took me, he was not far away. Many soldiers fear him; I too feared him as a young recruit. Numerous encounters taught me better, even to welcome him.

I saw friends, comrades, my brothers in arms, riddled with bullets and torn apart by shrapnel; saw the essence of life flowing out of them.

His breathing, which became heavier until the breath of life left him.

So many ... and almost all of them were afraid of the end.

No matter what faith or non-faith they adhered to, in the end, they feared and were afraid to follow the last companion. Not surprisingly, because God or even gods no longer find themselves on the battlefields of men, as it was so often told in the ancient sagas. Humans alone now create the deadliest means to slaughter and destroy each other. In nothing is the human mind so creative as destroying its own kind – the more cruel and effective, the better.

From the first prehistoric hunters who fought wars for better hunting grounds to the resource conflicts of the 21st century, one thing has always remained the same: man seeking to destroy man to gain an advantage.

Selfish, radical, consistent to the point of self-destruction, man is constantly looking for better ways to take what is most valuable from his neighbor in order to enrich himself.

This will not change. It is human nature.

As unpleasant as this essential realization may be, man is not the most effective predator that nature created, but the most deadly! With his ability to create tools of death, he is superior to natural predators.

Even if we were to explore the vastness of space in the distant future, we are talking about the conquest of it.

Without a doubt, my old friend will also follow us humans out there and be close to them as he has always been, from the beginning of human life.

The greed that is inherent in all people will not disappear from their souls, despite their protestations.

It is part of humanity, of human history, of every single human being. It is part of our DNA, our fundamental building blocks, and thus unchangeably anchored in our innermost being.

Once this has been accepted, conflicts suddenly appear explainable, comprehensible, understandable...

Man is born to fight. It is part of his nature, his fundamental structure. Even people who consider themselves peace-loving and loudly proclaim this are basically waging war. The fight for ideals can be judged as an act of war without further ado, even if people concerned would vehemently contradict this. Especially if they try to convince other people of their point of view. Being a peace activist is also a kind of war.

As bitter as this may be for those affected.

Ultimately, the whole of life is a single struggle. Beginning with birth, when the child tries to get out of the mother's womb and labors for the first breath, up to the last breath, which we humans often try to delay by all means.

These findings may be surprising, but they are the result of a life of struggle.

As a warrior/soldier, you fight for others' goals. Rarely do they coincide entirely with your own ideals or desires; sometimes, they even run completely counter to them.

You have to live with that, even if it is often challenging.

It is far more challenging to live with the faces of those you were forced to take their lives. Or the faces of the many friends and comrades whom you watched die without being able to do anything about it.

They are the ones who appear in your dreams at night and call out to you: Why?

Why did I have to die?

Why did you do this to me?

Why did you let me die?

Why did you take my life?

Questions to which the answers are as painful as the questions themselves.

Fulfillment of duty?

Self-defense?

Helplessness?

This does not lessen the guilt ...

How much suffering has accumulated over the centuries, the millennia of human history? The magnitude should be unimaginable.

The first war we know of took place about 5,500 years ago in the ancient city of Hamoukar in far northeastern Syria, not far from the Iraqi border. Here an early civilization, quite uncivilized, fought a great battle against an unknown enemy.

Wars probably existed earlier, but writing had not yet been invented, and we have no archaeological evidence to support this.

But that could very well still come.

As long as there have been people, war and therefore death has not been far away. I have fought in wars and conflicts of all kinds; no matter what they were called, they were all cruel, deadly, and full of unimaginable human excesses.

The ordinary person cannot imagine what his fellow species are capable of in extreme situations. Those who have seen it never forget it for the rest of their lives. Even if they would like to do so. Quite a few of those affected break up inwardly, mentally. The soul falls ill or even dies an agonizing death because the mind cannot process what people are capable of.

That's what happens to a lot of veterans.

Civilians are often alienated when former soldiers flinch at a loud noise or take up defensive positions when someone approaches them too quickly; when they startle loudly screaming from their sleep at night, or stare apathetically at something that seems utterly inconsequential to the average observer.

These are moments in which they repeat what they have experienced in their minds; they go through a rollercoaster ride of emotions, even to the point of shock. No one who has not personally smelled the gunsmoke and witnessed the deafening sounds of a battlefield can comprehend this. Explosions shake the body to the core. Every cell is filled with tension as adrenaline floods the veins. You react, mechanically reeling off the trained routines of combat stored in body and muscle memory. Aim, shoot, load, change position, aim, shoot, load, repeatedly until the enemy retreats or is destroyed.

He who thinks is dead, he who hesitates is dead, he who is too slow is dead!

Intense, violent, outside any norm.

Then the end of the fight. The body is still flooded with stress hormones, almost into an adrenaline rush. The images are perceived much more intensely. They are burned into your brain as if with a red-hot iron.

You see the mutilated and bleeding corpses of your own comrades and the bloody bundles of your killed enemies. The body tells you to keep fighting, but you force yourself to rest. Still, under the impression of the disturbing environment and the battle you just fought, you try to normalize your own condition so you can do your job. The wounded must be cared for, the dead recovered, the enemies searched for information and weapons.

If you experience this hellfire often enough, you become numb, your own sensations die out. You feel only a little, in the worst case, nothing anymore.

This often carries over into private life. You distance yourself from your confidants, your family. These often react with incomprehension because they do not realize that the person who has come back to them is not the same who left them, even if he appears outwardly unchanged.

It is more evident in external wounds; when limbs are missing, scars can be seen. But just as bad, if not worse, are the wounds on the soldier's soul, not visible, but just as painful and formative as any other injury and mutilation of the body. These are the consequences that many soldiers suffer, sometimes without realizing it themselves. This fate also befell me. I repressed the consequences, just carried on.

Nevertheless, the faces haunt me as well. If I ever end up in an afterlife, I will ask them if they forgive me or at least understand why I had to do what I did. I can only hope so.

I no longer fear death. I have encountered him in too many variations, and I respect him. That is the only way I have survived this long.

Respect for death may seem strange, but on closer inspection, it is not so strange. Death can't help it. He is just doing his job; we as humans and therefore every one of us is responsible for his actions and, therefore, his demise.

Now, as my own lifeblood seeps from my wounds into the soil of a foreign land and literally peters out there, I have made my peace with my old companion and comrade. I feel him approaching. He comes with silent but energetic steps, and I do not think of my end.

My thoughts are for my comrades, the men who stood beside me in battle, the friends and brothers for whom, in reality, I always fought. Not for my country or political ideas, not for ideologies or money. It was always the man to my left or right who made me fight to the last. My last wish is for those comrades whom I tried to buy time to escape. I wish that my last act was not unsuccessful. As my gaze veils and my old friend embraces me, I welcome him. My comrades will continue the fight as our forefathers did and their forefathers, for eons ...

Glossary

Ami: German nickname for a US-American. This is a term that is used totally neutrally. It does not have a negative or even slur connotation.

Bo-105: Multi-purpose helicopter by Messerschmitt-Bölkow-Blohm that was equipped with long-range anti-tank missiles for the Bundeswehr.

Braids (aiguillette): In the German army, all branches have their own shoulder-strap aiguillette (braid) color. Jägers, for example, wear green braids, tankers, pink braids, and so on. At the end of the three-month basic training, recruits are promoted to "Gefreiter" (= Private First Class) and receive their braids.

Bund: Commonly used short form for Bundeswehr

Bundeswehr: German Armed Forces, found in 1955 as former Western Germany's contribution to the North Atlantic Alliance. In 1990 the reunification with the soviet-controlled German Democratic Republic had the Bundeswehr absorb the GDR's National People's Army. Today the Bundeswehr consists of a civil administerial part and six military branches: the Army (=Heer), the Navy (=Marine), the Air Force (=Luftwaffe), the Joint Support Service (=Streitkräftebasis), the Joint Medical Service (=Zentraler Sanitätsdienst der Bundeswehr) and the Cyber and Information Space Command (=Kommando Cyber- und Informationsraum).

Comrade: This was a hard one for us. In the German military, the term "Kamerad" (plural = "Kameraden") is commonly used to address fellow soldiers; at the same time, communists and social democrats call themselves "Genosse" in German. There is only the one word, "comrade," in English, and it often has a communistic touch. I guess a US-soldier would not call his fellow soldiers "comrade"? Since the word "Kamerad" is very, very common in the German military, we decided to translate it with "comrade," but do not intend a communistic meaning in a German military context.

Deutsche Mark: Official currency of Western Germany and then unified Germany until it was replaced by the Euro in 2002.

Flakpanzer Gepard: It is a German anti-aircraft tank built by Krauss-Maffei as the prime contractor. It is armed with a pair of 35 mm autocannons and makes use of radar. The Bundeswehr started to phase out this weapon system after 2010. Other former or current operators include Belgium, the Netherlands, and Brazil. The Gepard is very popular among German soldiers and military fans; many of them grieved over the decision to phase it out of service.

Herr: Mister (German soldiers address sex AND rank, meaning they would say "Mister sergeant" instead of "sergeant")

Jäger: German military term referring to light infantry. Today the term is used very broadly. You have Gebirgsjäger for mountain troops, Fallschirmjäger for paratroopers, Panzerjäger for the Wehrmacht's anti-tank artillery. Jäger also refers to private and professional hunters.

Kamerad/Kameraden. See Comrade

Leopard 1A5: It is a German main battle tank and predecessor to the currently used Leopard 2 tank.

M113: US-American armored personnel carrier in service in the US Army and the German Army, among others. The mortar carrier of this story was equipped with a Soltam K6 mortar.

MIM-23 Hawk: Medium range surface-to-air missile system. In the Cold War, NATO set up Hawk positions all along the inter-German border. In the case of war, German and US Hawk units were supposed to occupy those positions and repel enemy aircraft attacks.

Mustering: The Federal Republic of Germany had conscription from 1956 to 2011. Therefore all male German citizens were invited to go through a mustering somewhere around their 18th birthday. At the mustering, which was obligatory for everyone, it was checked to see if one was capable of serving in the Bundeswehr. After World War 2, the Germans had the right to refuse to fight into their new constitution. Thus male Germans could choose between military service and public service.

Nordlicht: A German from northern Germany

Barracks-room: Since the Bundeswehr slang uses a very old German word to address the rooms where the soldiers live and sleep inside the barracks ... a word that no German civilian younger than 40 would possibly utter, we tried our best to save this mannerism by finding a similar English expression. Et voila: barracks-room. By the way, the German word is Stube.

Pencil Warriors: German military slur nickname for soldiers working in the headquarters.

Recovery Tank 2: When the Bundeswehr was founded, it very much relied on weapon systems provided by its Allies. At first, the US-American recovery tank M88 was procured and used under its German name "Bergepanzer 1". In the late 50's Germany began to develop its own military systems again on a large scale; the Leopard 1 battle tank was one successful outcome from those efforts. With the Leopard, the Bundeswehr began to develop an overall tank strategy. Learning from the mistakes made in World War 2, as many as possible, tank types were to be built on a single frame to keep costs low and create synergies. The Recovery Tank 2 is based on the Leopard chassis and was developed by Porsche.

Schupfnudel: Very thick noodle

Serviceableness: When the Federal Republic of Germany conscripted her young men, all had to go through the mustering, where their level of serviceableness was assessed on a scale from T1 to T6. T1 means one can work in all positions the Bundeswehr has. T6 means one is not able to do military service at all.

Spiess. Soldier's slang for Kompaniefeldwebel, the one NCO in a company responsible for all personnel matters and general order. In the German language, it is written with a "ß" = Spieß.

Stabsunteroffizier: There is more than one "sergeant rank" in the Bundeswehr. Unteroffiziers are promoted to Stabsunteroffiziers; both are OR-5 according to the NATO comparative military ranks, and both are translated as "sergeant."

Swabian pockets: Also, Maultaschen; describes pasta pockets filled with meat or spinach.

Temporary soldier: In the Bundeswehr, you have three different types of military service: respectively, draft service / voluntary service of up to 23 months; then temporary military service between 2 and 20 years (Zeitsoldat), and last but not least professional service (Berufssoldat) that lasts till retirement. You cannot apply for professional status initially, but first, you have to become a temporary service member.

Uhlan: Light cavalry

Unimog: A series of medium trucks produced by Daimler (Mercedes)

Unteroffizier: This one is tricky. On the one hand, it is a German army rank, NATO-Code OR-5, and comparable to a US-Sergeant. On the other hand, it also refers to two clusters of ranks: Unteroffizier ohne Portepee for all junior NCOs and Unteroffizier mit Portepee for all senior NCOs.

Volkswagen Iltis: It is a German military open jeep and predecessor to the Mercedes Wolf.

W15: W means Wehrpflicht (meaning conscription). The number stands for the months a draftee had to serve. When Schober joined the Bundeswehr, conscription demanded 18 months of service; his father had to serve for 15 months.

Wachbataillon: Meaning guard battalion; the Wachbataillon is the elite drill unit of the Bundeswehr. Its primary task is to perform military honors during state visits or similar events. The Wachbataillon is the only German military formation that still uses the old bolt-action K98k, which was the Wehrmacht's standard weapon. The K98k is not used for combat purposes but only for drills.

Wehrmacht. Unified armed forces of the Third Reich, consisting of Army (=Heer), Navy (=Kriegsmarine), and Air Force (=Luftwaffe). The Wehrmacht was dissolved in 1946 after Germany had surrendered unconditionally.

Y-Tours: A nickname for Bundeswehr referring to the fact that most soldiers travel around a lot and get to see different barracks in all corners of Germany and beyond. The Y takes into account that license plates of Bundeswehr vehicles always start with the letter Y.

EK-2 Publishing proudly presents

November 1942. Adolf Hitler, the "Führer" of the German Reich, unexpectedly dies in a plane crash in Hungary. The German High Command takes over the regime, disempowers the Nazi Party, and reorganizes the military forces. Germany swiftly has to overcome recent setbacks in North Africa and on the Eastern Front. Furthermore, an allied invasion already casts its long shadow. The German generals understand that it is not about ultimate victory anymore but merely about achieving a stalemate to save the Reich at the negotiating table. First, they have to stabilize Germany's positions on the Eastern Front. Therefore, the High Command gathers its panzer forces and throws them into a daring all-or-nothing gamble for the city of Kursk.

Get your copy of this complete and unique textbook about the famous German post-war main battle tanks Leopard 1 and Leopard 2!

The cover art was painted by German military painter Lucas Wirp

www.militaria-arts.de

Published by EK-2 Publishing GmbH
Friedensstraße 12, 47228 Duisburg, Germany
Registry court: Duisburg, Registry court ID: HRB 30321
Chief Executive Officer: Monika Münstermann

E-Mail: info@ek2-publishing.com

All rights reserved
Cover art: Lucas Wirp
Cover: Rock_0407
Authors: Hartmut Schober & Tom Zola
Translated from German by Jill Marc Münstermann
Final editing: Jill Marc Münstermann
Proofreading: Jesshay

Paperback ISBN: 978-3-96403-139-6
E-Book ISBN: 978-3-96403-138-9
Hardcover ISBN: 978-3-96403-140-2

1. Edition, March 2021

Manufactured by Amazon.ca
Bolton, ON